GRACES LIFE

how the adventure began

For information contact :
author.makenziecarpenter@gmail.com

Book Cover design by : Rian Gordon
Editor : Christopher Bigelow
Proofreading by : Hannah G. Scheffer-Wentz, English Proper Editing Services
ISBN: 979-8-9921604-0-6

First Edition: March 2025

10 9 8 7 6 5 4 3 2 1

GRACE'S LIFE

how the adventure began

BY MAKENZIE CARPENTER

To my amazing parents. My biggest supporters, my cheerleaders, my advocates.

CHAPTER 1

Everyone has a story. Nobody can tell me otherwise. Your journey to this point in life has been filled with hardship.

The only difference between you and me is the fact that I'm reliving these memories while you—if you're like most people—scurry away from yours. I relish being uncomfortable.

Do I feel proud about certain things I've accomplished? That depends. I'm proud to say that saving the world is my greatest accomplishment.

Curious to know about my journey and the challenges I have overcome?

If you are, there is something crucial I need to tell you. You are going to want to buckle up.

Hold on tight because this story is going to be wild.

■■■■■■■■■■■■■■■■■■

A tall, muscled sixteen-year-old boy dashed into the streets. Platinum-blond hair flying in the fierce, icy breeze as he ran.

Heart pounding in his chest like a wild bird aspiring to be free.

His legs. They were aching after fifteen minutes of running through downtown Dallas, Texas.

Sprinting beside the towering buildings, he caught the enticing aroma of flowers and food in nearby shops.

Taking a quick glance behind him, he saw that the lanky man with mischievous eyes continued to follow him. Fear engulfed him as he ran for his life. His mind flashed to the scenes of torture that would happen if he stopped running and allowed Stephen to catch up.

The boy had already noticed he was slowing down. His fast sprint was becoming more of a jog. He was growing tired, wanting to rest his aching legs for a minute.

He realized he had to escape from Stephen as quickly as possible.

I must locate her and inform her of the danger she is in.

The boy continued, pushing himself forward across a busy street.

At that exact moment, a red sports car came towards him at a snail's pace.

Like an action hero, he slid on his rear across the hood without another thought.

The car's shrill, deafening horn blasted. Landing on his feet, he kept on sprinting, glancing back to see if Stephen was still pursuing him.

He entered a crowded area. People were shouting and cursing at him as he pushed past them. The boy didn't care what anyone thought about him—if he began caring again, the hurtful comments would be his downfall. He needed to be strong and keep up his character as a teenager without emotions.

Lungs burning, breaths short and uneven, aching everywhere, his body screamed at him to stop. Despite everything, his mind urged him to continue.

I'm not ready to quit just yet. I have to tell her everything. She needs to know.

The boy continued to run across the road, toward an older part of Dallas.

After rounding the chipped-away corner of an old, abandoned apartment building, he pressed his body against the wall. His legs were unsteady from running.

Taking a couple of deep breaths, he listened. After a while, he heard someone run up the street and then stop nearby.

"I don't know where Jordan is, Grant!" Stephen's voice said, presumably into his phone. "Two old ladies blocked me when I reached for him. By the time I got my bearings, he was already gone! Let's hold off on telling Dr. Adrian that Jordan is gone."

Stephen's voice went quiet for a moment. Then he said, "I understand this messes with your plan to gain control over both Jordan and Dr. Adrian. Dr. Adrian's plan to take over the world hinges on Jordan's presence, which Jordan now recognizes. Without you, Grant, or him, Dr. Adrian is nothing. I didn't mean for Jordan to find out our plans."

I need to find a way into this building. Stephen could still catch me if I don't start moving.

Jordan crept along the old apartment wall as Stephen

continued speaking with Grant.

Not far ahead, a fire-escape ladder was fixed to the wall.

I should be able to climb up and hide in an apartment until Stephen is gone.

Grabbing the ladder's bottom rung, he hoisted himself up and started climbing. His body screamed at him to stop and rest. Sweat blurred his vision, but he kept on climbing.

A third of the way up, Jordan slipped into a memory from the past.

Why do I have to remember things at the worst moment?

With no energy to push away the memory, he let it come rushing back into his head.

He was in a noisy shopping mall. Looking back, he saw Stephen and one of Stephen's comrades close behind, maintaining an eye on him. Dr. Adrian allowed Jordan to leave the corporate building only if two bodyguards accompanied him.

He decided to ditch his bodyguards. Ducking into a shoe store, he lost himself among a crowd of kids. "Excuse me, ma'am," he said, summoning an employee. "Is your manager here today?"

"Yes, he is." The employee gave Jordan a curious look. "Let me go get him for you."

I hope Stephen doesn't decide to come in here. This might be my only chance to escape.

Moments later, a short, stout, balding man appeared. "One of my employees said you wanted to talk to me?" The man had a thick German accent.

"I'm hoping you can help me." Jordan suddenly worried how the manager would respond. He knew he was taking an enormous risk by telling a stranger about his problems. "I'm being pursued by dangerous men. Does this store have a back exit?"

To Jordan's surprise, the manager pointed without hesitation to a door. "If you go through there and down the stairs, there's an alleyway out back," he said in a hushed voice. "If anything happens to you, call my personal number and we'll help you out." He handed Jordan a business card.

Nodding in thanks, Jordan hurried to the door, trying not to draw attention to himself.

The memory ended. Still climbing the ladder, Jordan found himself outside an apartment's window. He tried to open it but could not.

Just then, he heard intense shouting from below. Startled, he looked down and saw at least ten cops. They were all training their guns on him.

Stephen or Grant must have called the cops on me. If Adrian finds out I'm gone, they could lose their jobs and that would scrap their precious plan.

Jordan looked for a way out, but there wasn't one.

He felt bitter disappointment. He wanted to get out of here, away from Stephen, away from Grant, and especially away from Dr. Adrian. He wanted to get away from his past life and make a fresh start.

An officer called out to Jordan again, "We have you trapped, Jordan! Climb down from the fire escape, place your hands behind your head, and kneel on the ground."

Thanks for stating the obvious. I can see you have me trapped. Jordan was thankful the policeman couldn't read his mind or else the officer would know he was sassing him.

As Jordan was climbing down the ladder, he saw Stephen

lurking in the shadows, phone in hand and a dark smile on his face.

I was correct. He was the one who called the cops.

Jordan pushed against the cops who surrounded him. Two of them tried to pin him to the ground, but Jordan wouldn't go down.

Where in the world did all this strength come from?

Two more men rushed to help their comrades pin down Jordan. He tried to fight against the four policemen, but the extra strength was leaving him.

The circle of policemen grew smaller and tighter as they all pressed in around him. After a moment, Jordan slumped to the ground, feeling defeated. He was too tired to fight back or struggle more.

One of the policemen patted Jordan down. "He's not armed. Everyone can relax."

Four of the officers surrounding Jordan lowered their guns, while two kept their guns trained on him. "Jordan Thurgood," said one of the big, burly men pinning him down. "We have a warrant for your arrest. You have the right to remain silent. Anything you say can and will be used against you . . ."

After the Miranda rights, Jordan was hoisted onto his feet, arms pinned against his back.

I was so close to getting away from Stephen and the entire Adrian Corporation. I was one step closer to finding my twin. Now my plan is being pushed further and further away from me.

To avoid crying in front of the policemen, he tried to emotionally withdraw from the situation. He needed to distract himself.

Just then, a policeman stood in front of Jordan. "Do you

recognize me?" the man asked with a slight smile. "Yes, you do—your expression says it all."

"There wouldn't be any point in saying I know you, Jeremiah," Jordan said.

"You didn't want to call me by my name, so you kept silent," Jeremiah murmured, stepping closer to Jordan. "Am I right, old pal?"

Jordan felt the policeman standing behind him shift his weight from one leg to the other, gauging this unknown situation.

They don't know what's going on. I'm assuming none of the other officers know our history.

"You think you know me so well, don't you," Jordan said.

"At one point, I did," said Jeremiah. "You rescued me from the fire in my Florida apartment. You helped me when no one else did. You and I ran wild together for a long time, keeping each other alive. Until we got arrested." Then Jeremiah's voice dropped to a deadly whisper. "You saved me from the wrath of Dr. Adrian—you took my place instead."

"That was the old me," growled Jordan, jerking forward towards Jeremiah. "Back when I cared about people."

Jeremiah stepped back, looking stunned. "You still care about people, Jordan. I know you do. Why else would you try to find your sister after all these years? Yes, I know what your plan was. You've had the plan since you found out she's alive."

Jordan opened his mouth in surprise.

"If you didn't care, you wouldn't be carrying around this necklace from your parents." Jeremiah lifted the dog-tag necklace around Jordan's neck.

He's blinded by his weakness in looking for the good in everyone. I have nothing left in me.

"I don't believe you murdered anyone or stole anything," Jeremiah said in Jordan's ear, "but that's why we're here to arrest you. They're charging you with theft and murder. You can prove to the judge that you're innocent. Prove that Dr. Adrian and his corrupt corporation are at fault, not you. You'll finally have the chance to tell the judge what Adrian has done to you all these years. Someone will finally solve the cold case of your disappearance. Your parents will be proud of you for your courage."

"That's what I'm being accused of, then?" Jordan asked. "Theft and murder?"

Jeremiah nodded. Someone behind Jordan coughed, and suddenly, the nice Jeremiah was gone. He started acting like a policeman again.

Jordan was not surprised at Jeremiah's comment, but it still angered him. *I've never murdered before in my life. Yes, I've stolen things here and there, but I had to survive somehow while living on the streets. Nobody was going to give me a job.*

Glancing over at where he'd seen Stephen standing, Jordan wasn't surprised that he was gone. *Grant must have told Stephen to leave the scene before the police saw him. He didn't need to be there anymore since I'm now in the government's hands.*

They escorted him to a police car and took him to the police station.

■■■■■■■■■■■■■■■■■■

Adrian Corporation was in a state of chaos.

"Did the police apprehend Jordan yet?" Grant demanded into the phone as he leaned back in his red, velvet roller chair.

"Yes, and he knows an officer," Stephen said. He was in his car, driving back to Grant in Montana. "They had a nice long chat, reliving their past for all I know. I couldn't hear anything."

"Let me guess, the police officer Jordan knows is a person named Jeremiah," Grant said.

"I don't know," Stephen admitted.

"Describe him to me."

"Uh—okay." Stephen sighed, trying to remember any details about the police officer.

"I'm waiting, Stephen. The day's not getting any younger, you know."

"Give me a second, Grant. I'm trying to remember what he looked like." Stephen pinched the bridge of his nose. "Now I remember!"

"Good for you," said Grant. After a few seconds, he continued, "Are you going to tell me what you remember or are you going to say you remember, but share no details?"

"Oh right, sorry," Stephen said. "Jeremiah's skin is an olive color. He has brown eyes. The sides of his head are shaved, and he has brown cropped hair on top."

Grant was silent for a moment. "Yes, I know exactly who he is. Jordan substituted for Jeremiah as the superhuman test subject. I never found out what happened to Jeremiah after he was released."

Grant's phone beeped. "Hold on, Stephen. I have to take this call." With a disgusted tone, he added, "Adrian is on the phone."

Not waiting for Stephen to respond, Grant hung up.

"Have you found that boy yet?" Adrian asked Grant. Wearing a nice suit, he was sitting impatiently at his desk. When he wanted things done, he wanted them done right away. That's why his company was successful.

When Adrian was a young boy, he'd aspired to be a businessman and run his own company. But his peers mocked him because they'd never heard of someone from a poor family creating a successful business from just an idea. When he was older, Adrian directed his schooling and studies towards becoming a business major. Once his peers found out what Adrian was accomplishing, they all aspired to be part of his success.

But Adrian had turned people down left and right. He knew his peers just wanted to ride on his success, and he would not let them do that when they'd all initially thought his idea for building a science and technology company would fail. Adrian wanted only the best people fit for the tasks that needed to be completed. He'd thoughtfully hired scientists, doctors, nurses, guards, customer service consultants, designers, and engineers. He'd also ended up expanding Adrian Corporation into espionage, with spies located all over the world. He trusted every one of his workers and held them in the highest regard. They'd built powerful businesses together based on trust and reliability.

At first, Adrian had thought only of helping combat diseases that other scientists couldn't solve. At this point in his life, however, he wanted to earn even more money and increase his power in the world.

Adrian had grown fond of Jordan over the years. The boy was like a son to him. But it made him very anxious when he had to stop business to handle the boy. Rubbing his graying hair, he waited for Grant to answer his question.

On the other end of the line, Grant gulped. *Well, I had everything handled before you poked your nose where it didn't belong. I got Jordan off the streets before any civilians could figure out his link to Adrian Corporation. Adrian will figure out I'm the one running this business, once he looks past his greed and ego.*

"No, sir, we haven't yet," he said to Adrian, avoiding telling his impatient boss about the boy's arrest. The less Adrian knew, the better. "Why in the world would he disappear?"

Dr. Adrian was quiet for a moment. "Jordan could've been unhappy being stuck by my side and hidden in my shadow. I have no definite explanation for his disappearance."

"Jordan's a very tricky boy to handle, from what I've observed over the past couple years working for you. I don't know how you can handle him," Grant said.

"Jordan respects me. But he acts like his rebellious father, and he has his father's temper."

"Everyone in this corporation respects you, sir. I don't understand the need to find Jordan. He could be dead on the side of the road." Grant's patience was wearing thin.

"I already know everyone respects me, but that's because I'm their boss." Dr. Adrian sounded frustrated. "There's no doubt in my mind that Jordan is still alive. I want you to set up four large search teams all over Texas."

"Okay, I can do that. I'll also set up search teams for Jordan's missing twin sister."

"What do you mean, twin sister?" Dr. Adrian's voice grew interested.

Crap. I wish I hadn't brought up the twin sister. "You never knew Jordan had a sister?" Grant asked, sounding as shocked as possible.

"No, I didn't. I assumed Jordan was the only person still alive after his family was murdered and their house was burned down. Jordan doesn't talk about his past life with me. Whenever I bring it up, he shuts me out and gets all defensive, sometimes for several days. I've learned what boundaries I can't cross."

Grant leaned back in his office chair, fiddling with a pen. "Using the blood tests when Jordan was first found, researchers looked all over the country for known relatives. Jordan and his twin sister, Grace, are the only two people still alive in their family."

"Since nobody reported Jordan missing, I'd assumed he had no living relatives," Dr. Adrian said. "But now you finally see fit to inform me otherwise."

"I was about to talk about Grace," said Grant. "From what I can gather, she and Jordan were separated after their parents and older brother were murdered. Grace has been jumping from foster family to foster family. By their thirteenth birthdays, Jordan and Grace were on opposite ends of the country. She's been in the foster system since about the time you rescued Jordan from the streets."

"Sounds like you have the Grace investigation under control. But how long were you going to hide Jordan's arrest from me?" Dr. Adrian's voice changed from carefree to condescending.

How does he know about Jordan getting arrested? Then the truth hit Grant like a sledgehammer. Dr. Adrian had sent spies to watch Stephen.

"Your silence speaks volumes to me," Dr. Adrian said.

"I was waiting for the right time to tell you," Grant responded.

"Dishonesty isn't a pretty color on you, Grant."

"I'm shocked that you don't trust Stephen or me. Instead of talking civilly like adults, you sent a spy to snoop on my personal business." *Now I can't hide Jordan or what I find out about Grace.*

"You're getting into dangerous territory there, Grant," Dr. Adrian said. "Out of all people, you should know that Jordan is my business. Whatever happens to Jordan, I take seriously and personally."

Grant angrily pulled the phone away from his ear, then returned it. "Actually, I misspoke, sir," he said, gritting his teeth.

"What do you mean then, Grant?"

"I meant to say, I didn't know how to break the news to you that Jordan escaped and got arrested." The lie came out easily. *Please believe it, Adrian.*

Dr. Adrian's voice grew softer. "You could've told me straightforwardly that Jordan got arrested. The news hurts me either way, but if you had the courage to tell me, the blow would not be as harsh."

"I completely understand," Grant replied. "But I feel I made the right call in not telling you about Jordan getting arrested."

"How can that be the right call?" Dr. Adrian interrogated.

"Because you need to focus all your energy on your upcoming press conference, and you can't do that if your mind is muddled with Jordan's situation."

"Hmm, I see your point," said Dr. Adrian. "But my gut tells me something isn't adding up."

"I completely understand," said Grant. "But once you have time to think my words over, you'll agree with me."

"Now that we've gotten Jordan's situation up to date, let's talk about a new issue," said Dr. Adrian. "Have you been able to track down this . . . Grace?"

"At one point, my team of twenty highly experienced satellite hackers and ten field spies had all eyes on her. But a couple months ago, she suddenly disappeared and we can't find her anywhere."

"What you're telling me, Grant, is that the girl is lost," Dr. Adrian stated.

"No, sir. Remember, we still have Jordan to be our tracker if we need. Grace is only one step away from being right where you want her."

"Grant, with Jordan being in police custody, he can't track Grace down."

"I'll have my search teams keep looking for her," Grant said, sitting back in his office chair. "One of my agents will find her again."

"Good. With a handful of luck, we'll get Jordan back and have him track Grace as soon as possible." After a pause, Dr. Adrian continued, "Well, I'll let you continue doing whatever I stopped you from doing." He hung up.

Sighing angrily, Grant pulled at his hair and then turned on his computer and typed in his password.

CHAPTER 2

Grace shivered from the cold as the wind continued to blow. Looking through her backpack, she realized she didn't have anything to withstand the cold or the wind.

Some passersby looked at Grace with sympathy. Others didn't look in her direction at all, but down at the shiny phones in their hands.

Tears pricked the corners of her eyes and she brushed them away angrily. *Crying won't do me any good—even more people will stare at me. I have to figure out a way on my own.*

The last hope Grace had was now gone. She knew that if her own family hadn't found her by now, they wouldn't ever find her.

She thought back to a couple days ago, when this disaster had begun.

Grace lived on a street with pristine yards and large, fancy, modern houses with top-of-the-line appliances and technology. She suspected that the people living in these homes spent much of their time spying on their neighbors and judging them. They were all snobs, never associating with anybody who wasn't rich or famous.

Grace disliked them all, including the family she was currently living with, with one exception. She'd started living with this family when she was thirteen, and now she was sixteen. Her two foster brothers and two foster sisters were all older than her.

Only Elijah actually had a kind heart and treated her like a person, not an object or someone to taunt and jeer at all the time. He helped her with cooking, laundry, chores, and homework. He and his friends included her in their activities even though she was younger.

Since she was little, Grace had been bounced from family to family like a puppy nobody wanted. She never felt like she belonged anywhere.

For the most part, her current foster family made sure she knew she was different and didn't belong. They reminded her every day that she wasn't loved and that they'd be happy for her to disappear.

Grace didn't have any friends. Whenever she was at school, her siblings would chase her classmates away so she couldn't make friends. Her family publicly made fun of her, and her siblings' friends joined in the fun of her public humiliation. At first, the comments hadn't bothered her, but as time went on, the constant rude comments and cruel reminders degraded her self-confidence.

Grace's family enjoyed seeing her in pain.

At night, she found solace with occasional flashbacks of her life with previous families.

In the earliest family she could remember, the dad worked some kind of government job and the mom worked at a bookstore. Grace and the two little girls would help out at the bookstore. Grace was able to read countless books. The parents showed their affection, making sure Grace was happy with them and actually caring about her. Grace couldn't remember exactly why she'd had to leave them.

The next family was a young couple with no kids except Grace. The couple had a border collie, and Grace still longed for that same breed of dog. However, she knew that if she tried asking her current family, they'd just say no and tell her she demanded too much. The young foster dad had worked for a software company and wasn't ever home. The mom taught at the school Grace had attended. They adored her so much—she was their pride and joy. Sadly, the mom and dad died in a car wreck. Grace was the only survivor, walking away unharmed.

Grace's next family wasn't kind to her. The parents both drank heavily, and the dad had an extremely bad temper. Their seventeen-year-old daughter was never home, always either at work or a friend's house. The dad would abuse Grace both mentally and physically. When the agency found out, they instantly removed her from that house. But most of the scars she still carried were from him, and his abuse had made her lose trust in people.

The next family helped Grace get through her recent traumas. They were patient and kind with her, made sure she was comfortable, and helped her adjust to her new life with them. Their oldest son and Grace got along quite well. The family also had twin girls. Grace got along with them too, but she preferred being with the older brother because he did what she liked to do in her spare time. Both the mom and dad were counselors at schools.

Two mornings ago, Grace was getting ready in her bedroom. *Today is three years since I joined this family, but I know they aren't going to do anything to celebrate. They never celebrate anything related to me.*

She could overhear some of her foster siblings yelling at their parents in the dining room. They didn't want to do homework or chores. They wanted their friends to come over more often for late nights. They didn't get new clothes every month like their friends did. The house was small compared to their friends' houses. To Grace, it seemed almost big enough to hold the extended family on both sides.

Grace hurriedly pulled on one of the few clean shirts she owned. *I better get going before they make a huge deal about how I didn't fix their breakfast.*

She glanced at the small mirror on her bedroom wall. Looking back was a slender, small-statured girl with long, straight, plain, brown hair, dull, green eyes, and pasty, white skin.

Sighing, Grace pulled her hair into a ponytail. *Another long day of being a slave and going to school, just to come back home and slave away again. My life is just the same charade over and over again. Nothing new ever happens.*

She crossed the room to the door, stomped down the elegant hallway, and ran down the stairs to the commotion below. *If only the parents were better at teaching their children, I'd probably be seen as an equal and my life wouldn't be as bad.*

Passing the living room, Grace saw Elijah sitting on a couch, his brows furrowed in concentration as he read something on his phone. *Well, at least he's not just staring out the window and saying rude comments about people walking past.* She'd noticed that Elijah tried to stay away from his family as much as possible.

As Grace neared the kitchen, dread crept over her. She didn't want to deal with her family today. She walked through the well-lit, spacious kitchen to the adjacent dining room, where five out of the family's seven members were seated at the table, waiting for Grace to make breakfast for them.

"What took you so long, Grace?" mocked her foster sister, Roxy.

Very rarely did Grace get up late, but when she did, they always said the same rude comments. *Once again, they could've made breakfast for themselves.*

Grace grumbled internally as three of her siblings said more mean comments to her because she was only *one* minute late making breakfast.

To Grace's relief, Elijah walked into the dining room and sat down by his two sisters. The family instantly stopped talking. He looked at his siblings one at a time, his lips drawn into a hard line and his eyes blazing with anger.

Elijah's countenance changed when he caught Grace's attention. He winked at her as she passed the table, all traces of anger gone from his eyes.

Elijah said, "Hey, everyone, I found discounted tickets for the Rock Dream Army concert tonight. Any of you want to go?"

After a moment of silence, loud chattering and chaos broke out again. Yes, everyone wanted to go.

"What will we wear?" cried Isabella.

All five jumped up and started running around the house, trying to get to their rooms. Grace stood in the doorway and Elijah sat at the table, both silently laughing as they watched.

The family members ran into each other on the way to their rooms. After some struggling, they all finally made it to their destinations. Grace heard four doors slam shut.

Elijah was still smiling. *Of course he'd be smiling. He just witnessed his family go crazy.*

"I can't believe how fast they went for that," commented Grace.

Elijah came over to the doorway. Slightly laughing, he said, "I kind of bluffed."

When Grace gave him a doubtful look, he added, "I *did* happen to find discounted tickets online, but I didn't buy them."

Grace laughed. "That'll make them mad. Of course, they'll blame me for the lie." While Elijah was considered the perfect child who could do no wrong, Grace always got yelled at for things she didn't do.

Elijah shrugged and was about to say something back, probably something witty or funny like always, but the conversation was cut short by everyone coming back into the dining room.

"Grace, when are those pancakes going to be done?" griped Isabella, who looked worse in the red dress she'd changed into. "I need to eat, like, right now, before I pass out from starvation."

The dress was too tight around Isabella's chest and hips, and it was way too short for her. Nonetheless, Grace wistfully looked at Isabella's clothes, then looked at her own plain, unflashy clothes.

Grace knew she shouldn't say anything about the change of clothes, so she replied, "They'll be ready in a minute."

Their father was looking suave and professional in a navy-blue suit and floral tie. Instead of responding to Grace, he rose from the table and said curtly, "Elijah, can I talk to you for a moment?"

"Of course," Elijah replied. As he left the dining room, he looked back at Grace with a worried expression.

"Have you applied for the job yet?" Elijah's dad whispered eagerly as they stood in the living room.

Of course he was going to ask that. He's been asking me about this for weeks.

"I haven't had time, nor was I going to apply for the guard position," Elijah said in a hushed voice. "I don't want to throw my life away."

As Elijah spoke, his stomach tied up in knots. He couldn't believe he'd admitted his feelings to his father. *Oh, great. He's about to throw a hissy fit because I'm not following his orders.*

"You better apply for the job or I'll kick you out of the house," Elijah's dad said sternly, his eyes communicating that he would follow through with his threat. Elijah knew that once his dad said he was going to do something, no matter how small the task was, he was going to complete it.

"You do realize I'm an adult, correct?" Elijah retorted. "I don't have to apply for the job if I don't want to. I want to do something beneficial with my life, something I'll actually enjoy."

"You *have* to apply. It's a really great-paying job." Elijah's dad sounded a bit too anxious and whiny.

"Then why don't *you* apply?" Elijah said bitterly. "I don't care how much I'll get paid. I've seen you and Mom care more about money than your own children—or really anybody, for that matter. And now Sam, Roxy, and Isabella are caring about money more than anything because they think it'll solve all their problems. But more money causes more problems. It only gives you short-term happiness, and I've seen it burn more friendships than I can count."

Elijah's dad smacked him hard on the face. "Don't you dare talk to your father like that. You were raised to care about money and fame, not about people's feelings and what'll happen to them."

What if I care about people more than I care about money and fame? Then would you say I've failed at learning your version of so-called life?

Elijah looked his dad straight in his cold eyes. "I told you what I want to do for a living. I'm not going to let you decide my future and what I can and cannot do."

"Well, you seem to have grown a backbone," Elijah's dad growled. He hit Elijah again, throwing him against the wall. Elijah hoped the family hadn't heard.

"Don't tell anyone what happened or you'll be punished much more severely," Elijah's dad said viciously. Then he walked back to the kitchen, acting like nothing had happened.

Like what you just did to me wasn't severe enough.

Watching the back of his dad's head, Elijah tried not to cuss at him or say something he'd regret later. He rubbed his face where his dad had struck him, then went into the bathroom and turned on the light.

There in the mirror, Elijah saw a young man who had no idea how to get out of the life he was living, how to help Grace not suffer the same fate, and how to hide the red welts on his face.

Elijah finally went back into the kitchen and watched Grace finish making the food. A few moments later, she carefully walked into the dining room, balancing a bunch of plates with pancakes on them.

Grace, please don't drop those plates, or your punishment could be worse than the one I just got.

Elijah felt a twinge of guilt creep up his body as he watched Grace struggling to keep all the plates from falling out of her arms and onto the floor. His heart was telling him to go help her, but his brain told him that his parents would punish him even more.

He slumped into his chair and let Grace continue with her work, pretending he didn't care. Guilt gripped every square inch of him and he regretted his decision not to do anything.

During breakfast, the family ate in silence.

Grace wasn't allowed to eat at the table with the rest of the family. She was fine with that, so she just stood in the kitchen and contentedly ate her meal.

My life could be a lot worse than what I'm going through right now. I could have no place to call home, no belongings instead of the few things I own, no clothing, and no food. This is better than nothing.

After finishing her meager meal she'd prepared for herself, she carefully set her dish into the sink, making sure she didn't break her parents' china plate.

I better see if everyone else is done with their plates so I can do the dishes.

She tightened her ponytail, made sure she appeared presentable, and walked down the steps to the dining room.

To her confusion, everyone was gone. An eerie silence had settled over the house.

That's really odd. Surely someone would've gotten my attention to tell me it was time to go. I'll just walk to school by myself, again.

Grace picked up the empty dishes and cups from the glass table, making sure she wouldn't drop them. Then she slowly made her way up the kitchen steps and set the dishes next to the sink.

As she worked, she hummed a song she remembered her birth mother singing to her so many years ago. The song made her feel a bit better.

Suddenly, she heard something fall in the living room. Turning around, she saw a man in black clothes and a black mask walking towards her.

What in the world?! Panicking, Grace hurriedly found a knife in the soapy water. Then she brandished it at the intruder, willing to do anything to protect herself. Her breath came in fast pants as adrenaline began coursing through her body.

Laughing harshly, the intruder rushed forward, pulled out a dagger, and took a swipe at Grace.

She quickly dropped to the floor and rolled to the left, away from her attacker.

His knife hit the stack of dirty dishes by the sink, causing them to shatter. The pieces rained down on Grace. She jumped up and moved away.

"Come back here," the attacker said, turning towards her.

Holding up the kitchen knife, Grace slowly backed down the steps into the dining room.

"I didn't realize you were going to fight back," the attacker said, sauntering toward her. "Otherwise, I would've brought my gun."

Grace backed into the dining table, which stopped her from getting any farther away. The attacker slowly got closer, waving the knife tauntingly. Grace knew she would have to fight back or get killed. She took a slow, deep breath.

Suddenly, another masked figure entered the room, clothed in black and holding a gun.

Fantastic, there's two attackers now! I'm going to freaking die.

But the second attacker turned his attention to the first attacker, not to Grace. The first man aimed his dagger and threw it at the second man.

At the same time, the gun went off, making Grace jump.

Blood erupted from the first attacker's chest. He fell to the ground and lay still.

There's no way this intruder killed my attacker.

The second man holstered his gun and turned to Grace.

Still holding up her knife, Grace quivered, knowing she was done for.

To her surprise, the intruder raised his hands in surrender, then carefully removed his black mask.

"Elijah!" she cried. "What're you doing here? I thought you all left for school and work. Who was that, and why did he try to attack me?" As she spoke, Grace's voice rose in concern. "And why are you dressed all in black?"

With a pained look on his face, Elijah moved toward her, opening his arms wide like he was going to hug her. Grace felt tears spring to the corners of her eyes.

"Grace," he managed to whisper in a sad voice. Tears started flowing down his face, but he made no movement to brush them away. His eyes held a million words and emotions, pain the most evident one she could see.

"Can you please just hug me one last time?" Elijah whispered, his body slightly shaking.

Grace tried to stifle her sobs as she hugged her brother. "What's going on?" she whispered, her voice breaking as she continued to sob.

"I was tasked to kidnap you and give you to a man who's obsessed with finding you," Elijah explained, worry in his voice. "I don't know why. I must follow orders, or you and I will be in a lot more trouble than we're already in. As for this other man, I have no idea who he is. All I know is that you're going to live another day. Everything's all right."

I don't know what's going on, but I do know that I trust Elijah.

"Grace, I have a few things to give you before I have to—" His voice broke, and a new round of sobs began.

They stood there in the dining room in each other's embrace, not saying anything.

"We don't have much time," Elijah finally said, pulling himself out of Grace's arms.

Grace nodded, hurriedly brushing tears out of her eyes.

Elijah led Grace through the living room, which was full of turned-over furniture, strewn books and papers, and shattered glass.

"What happened to this place?" Grace asked softly.

Elijah darkly grinned. "This was to show my appreciation to my parents. I hope I broke every valuable object I could."

"They'll sure enjoy cleaning up this huge mess," Grace commented, following Elijah upstairs.

Elijah laughed slightly as he led her to his room. Quietly closing the door, he moved past Grace to his desk. "The things I want to give you are in here," he explained, handing Grace a large yellow envelope.

Grace turned the envelope over, inspecting both sides. She was about to open it when Elijah said, "Grace, I want you to wait till I'm gone to open it. There are some things I don't want to be around for when you read them. I'm already in pain over the fact that I have to kidnap you. Please don't bring more pain upon me."

Grace nodded. "I promise I'll wait." She slipped the envelope into her shirt.

Elijah sighed with relief. "Good. We should be going. My partner will be wondering what's taking me forever."

Elijah handed Grace a blindfold. His other hand held a gag and some rope. "Put the blindfold on and I'll do the rest," he said kindly, tears shining in his eyes again. "Please trust me one last time, Gracie."

I can trust him one last time. He's the only person I care about. I don't want to see him get hurt. I hope this isn't really the last time I'll ever see him.

Grace slipped on the blindfold. Her eyesight was now completely gone.

Elijah gagged her and tied her hands, then he led her down the stairs.

"We're getting near the front door," Elijah whispered. "You still have the envelope?"

Grace nodded, her heart pounding in her ears. *Stay calm, Grace. Don't go losing your cool now. Just trust Elijah one last time.*

"Make sure my partner doesn't see the envelope, or this situation will get messy really fast," Elijah advised.

Grace nodded again. *There's no turning back now. I'm never going to return to this evil house. I'm never going to see this awful family again. I'm never going to be able to see Elijah again. I don't know what's going to happen to me, but I hope I don't die.*

When they were outside, she heard a booming voice ask skeptically, "Is this the girl the boss told us to kidnap?"

"Yes, this is the girl the boss wants," Elijah said, sounding defensive. He began carefully helping Grace into a vehicle.

His partner grumbled, "You're really taking time to make sure she's not harmed?"

Elijah didn't say anything, but his grip on Grace tightened as he continued helping her into the vehicle.

"You do know I'm talking to you, right?" mocked the man.

Elijah stopped helping Grace, and then she heard him say in a low, dangerous voice, "Did you know I have a gun on me, and it's loaded? I could shoot you right now and nobody would know what happened to you, let alone miss you."

"Can you please put the gun away?" the man said, his voice quaking.

Grace sensed that Elijah had moved away from her. "I really don't care if you mock me, hurt me, take me to the police, or try to get me fired," he said to his partner. "I have thick skin, and nothing hurts me anymore. If the one person I care about is getting insulted, then there's a problem. As long as you don't insult my sister again, I'll put my gun away."

"Okay," the man said. "I didn't realize how attached you were to this girl."

Elijah turned his attention back to helping Grace get into her seat. *I've never heard him that angry before. I didn't realize he cared so much about me that he'd threaten to kill someone.*

Just before Elijah shut her door, Grace heard his partner say something cruel about her. *Elijah, don't shoot the guy! Kidnapping me is only a job for the man. He's just here to get paid.*

With the door shut, Grace could still hear the men speaking loudly. Hard rock played at low volume on the radio, and the vehicle smelled like cleaning supplies and cigarette smoke. Her seat felt hard like a park bench.

After a few minutes, Elijah and his partner got into the vehicle. The ignition sounded and the vehicle started moving.

"Do you know where we're going?" Elijah asked, trying to make his voice casual.

His partner grunted. "Yes, the boss texted me the location."

The driver made a few turns, then increased the car's speed on what must have been a highway. Suddenly, Grace heard a metallic click and one of the men let out a surprised cry. She realized one of them had just cocked a gun's trigger.

What in the world is going on? Who's pointing that gun at who? She squirmed around in her seat in a panic.

"What're you doing, Elijah?" his partner asked. "I didn't insult your sister or do anything to offend you."

Grace could hear a smile in Elijah's voice as he said, "I don't work for that vile man you call a boss. You and everyone else in that company think my full trust is in someone who craves power more than he cares about his actual workers. You have no idea how hard my team and I have worked to make this day perfect. To finally get Grace into our hands and save her from your boss's cruel power game."

The gun fired and the car went into a screeching swerve.

CHAPTER 3

Jordan could tell he would be at the police station for a while.

He was taken to a concrete confinement cell and told that he would stay there until it was time for him to appear before a judge.

I'm surprised they didn't ask me more questions. I'm sure they'll ask me more tomorrow.

Jordan grimly stared off into space for a moment. Then he took out a crumpled piece of paper that he'd carefully placed into his orange jumpsuit and looked at it intently.

"I promised myself that I would protect you," Jordan muttered to himself, "but this is where I ended up instead." A vision entered his head of a previous time when he'd run away from pursuers, only to find himself incarcerated. Jordan tried to push the memory away, but it kept on coming into his mind. So finally, he just let it play.

■■■■■■■■■■■■■■■■■■

Jordan was walking through a park in the twilight. He tried to act as normal as he could, but he could sense someone was watching him.

He didn't want to run yet, but he increased his pace to a brisk walk.

Jordan pulled the collar of his leather jacket up closer to his face, as if to hide himself. With his other hand, he touched the dog-tag necklace his parents had given him long ago. Dr. Adrian had repeatedly told him that his real parents and his twin sister were dead. He knew it wasn't true, no matter how many times he heard the lie.

I'm not going crazy. I know someone is watching me.

Jordan heard footsteps stamping towards him. Spinning around on his heels, he saw a group of five boys coming straight at him. As they got closer, he realized they were gang members. They all had skull chains around their necks, they wore the same jackets, and they all walked a certain way. The area had a few gangs, but Jordan knew this was one of the gangs he'd been told to avoid.

The boy in the middle must be the gang leader.

Jordan watched the group from the corner of his eye. They were coming dangerously close. When they got near enough that he could see their eyes, he knew they wanted to kill him.

"Hey, blondie, how'd you get so ugly?" the gang leader asked, getting up in Jordan's face. "Your mom drop you in the gutter when you were a baby?"

"Oh, yeah?" spat Jordan. "Your haircut makes you look fat."

The gang leader got a little red in the face. "Get him," he said, his voice dead and cold.

The boys circled around Jordan. He swung his fists, but one of them came from behind. He twisted Jordan's arms behind his back and jerked his body forward.

The gang leader punched him, hard.

Jordan tried to lean forward onto his knees, but they pulled him back upright.

"That's what you get when you insult someone," the gang leader said with evil grin. "Maybe you'll learn a lesson or two by the time I'm done with you."

He looks like a creepy jack-in-the-box with yellow, crooked teeth.

Jordan's mind moved in a million different directions as he tried to come up with an escape plan.

My legs aren't pinned. I can kick the guy behind me and run away.

Jordan put his plan into action. He moved his leg up a little, then kicked back as hard as he could. He heard a loud *snap,* and someone cried out and then hit the ground.

Jordan threw a good punch at the gang leader and bolted towards the road.

He could hear feet pounding after him. Jordan had to get away from these people, but how?

That's when an idea came into his mind.

He turned a corner and started to backtrack into the park again. He still could hear the gang pounding after him. Jordan then changed his direction again and ran away from the park.

This is not how I imagined my day going.

After running for a couple minutes, he realized the gang wasn't following him anymore.

Jordan continued running, heading towards a large residential area.

He could feel his strength dwindling every second he spent walking.

Jordan finally collapsed on the side of the road. He could feel every bone in his body screaming out in pain. He lay back, closed his eyes, and drifted off.

Some unknown amount of time later, Jordan slowly opened his eyes and lifted his head. To his surprise and horror, he was in a different place. He was on a cot in the middle of a red room. Standing nearby was a man wearing all gray.

Where am I? Who's this guy?

"Hello, Jordan. My name is Dr. Adrian. I'm the CEO of Adrian Corporation. You're here because I need to keep you safe from the people who want to hurt you."

"Why are you trying to save me?" Jordan asked in confusion. "Nobody is after me."

"I saved your life," said Dr. Adrian. "You collapsed on the sidewalk from exhaustion. I had some tests done on you, and you're exactly the person I've been looking for."

Stop playing mind games and tell me what's really going on.

"What are you trying to tell me?" Jordan shouted. "Just spit it out!"

Dr. Adrian sighed. "You're more unique than anyone I've ever met. However, your temper is a bit off, you don't know how to really fight yet, and you don't have much schooling. I'm going to help you with those things."

Jordan followed Dr. Adrian out of his cell and into a spacious, empty room. Dr. Adrian told him to stand in the middle of the room. "All right, I'm going to teach you how to protect yourself when facing an opponent." The doctor paused, raising an eyebrow. "We'll see how well you do, and then we'll go on from there. Understood?"

Jordan nodded. Dr. Adrian gave him some additional instructions. At the doctor's signal, Jordan started running towards Dr. Adrian. Moments later, he found himself on the ground.

Dr. Adrian stood over him, shaking his head. "You're going to learn so much. The first thing I'll teach you is your stance. Now, on your feet."

Jordan practiced hour after hour, day after day, learning many new fighting techniques. Jordan's anger slowly rose with each day he had to spend throwing punches.

How much longer do I have to practice? By the time I'm done, I'll be twenty!

After being confined to the red room for months, Jordan was finally moved to a hotel-style room. He was also given access to certain parts of the building. On one outing, he ran into another boy named Jeremiah. They became fast friends and started conspiring to escape from Dr. Adrian.

After a year of training, Jordan's fighting stance was better, he'd learned to control his anger, and he'd mastered several fighting tactics and survival skills.

"You've done well. Now here's your test. I want you to kill him." Dr. Adrian pointed casually to a man tied to a chair in the middle of the room.

Jordan froze in his tracks. *How can I kill him? That's an innocent man.*

"I don't think I can. You've taught me well, but this is a human-being we're talking about. I don't want to kill him and shed innocent blood."

Dr. Adrian looked at him with an angry expression that conveyed: *Kill this man before I kill you.*

Jordan sighed and stepped back, still not wanting to kill the man.

Dr. Adrian glanced at Jordan and then at the man again. He started drawing his knife from the bag tied to his belt loop, but Jordan lunged at him, flinging the knife from Dr. Adrian's hand. Jordan then positioned himself in front of the bound man, trying to protect him the best he could.

"You're making a big mistake, boy. You said you would do anything I tell you. Did you lie to me when you took the oath?"

"You didn't tell me I would have to *kill* someone!" shouted Jordan, holding his own knife in the position Dr. Adrian had taught him.

He's trying to distract me. Jordan seemed to know what Dr. Adrian was thinking. Dr. Adrian had trained him well—maybe a little too well.

Dr. Adrian circled, looking for the best angle of attack. "Drop your knife before I kill you and this man," he said calmly.

"Make me!" Jordan shouted angrily. Whenever the doctor tried making a move, Jordan blocked him.

Dr. Adrian sighed and tried to reason with Jordan, but Jordan remained as stubborn as ever. Finally, Dr. Adrian threw down his knife in frustration. "Jordan, I give up. You're smarter and quicker than me. You and this man live. Don't make me regret my decision. Leave before I change my mind."

Dr. Adrian quietly stepped back and Jordan ran out the door as fast as he could, making sure he wasn't being followed. Dr. Adrian never came after him.

Jordan ran out of the building, towards the heart of the city. He didn't know if Dr. Adrian was going to come after him or not.

After a while, his stomach started to grumble. He didn't have any money. He entered a grocery store, heart pounding and blood rushing in his ears. He knew this wasn't the best decision, but he didn't have any choice. Starve and die, or steal some food and live.

He tried to act as calm as he could. After much debate, he decided on an assortment of crackers, cheese, meat, and bread.

With a deep inhale, Jordan ran past the sensors. The store alarms started to blare. Everyone in the store was trying to figure out what was going on.

Before Jordan could set foot out the door, cops surrounded him. There was no escape.

Well, so much for walking away without getting caught.

Jordan was cuffed, put in a police car, and taken to the youth detention center. He knew Dr. Adrian couldn't get him there. Dr. Adrian didn't know where Jordan had gone or what he was planning.

Jordan found himself in another cell with tight security. *How much longer will I have to be in jail?*

A while later, a police officer entered the cell. "Time to get up, Thurgood," he said.

The guard took Jordan to the outside yard, which was full of juvenile delinquents. *I'm going to stay far away from everyone. Otherwise, who knows what kind of trouble I'll get in?*

The walled enclosure wasn't much to look at. It held some exercise equipment and a few tables and chairs. Guards stood every few yards, carefully watching everything.

Jordan walked slowly around the yard. Most of the other boys didn't look at him twice. But one group kept their eyes on him. His heart started pounding in his ears.

Finally, one of the boys started to walk over towards Jordan.

I'm smelling trouble. I better be prepared for anything. Some of them may have ended up here for killing people.

Jordan carefully watched the boy approach. He was familiar with pecking orders, and he could tell this guy was the leader of this particular pecking order. Jordan did not feel alarmed.

"I heard you got into some trouble," the boy said casually. "What did you do to get yourself in here?"

"Yeah, I was in a tight spot." Jordan tried to match the boy's casual tone. "I stole food from a store not too far from here."

The boy nodded, smiling a little. He raised his hand towards Jordan, probably wanting to shake his hand or something.

I don't know what to do—he's a criminal. I'm just going to try getting some allies. This is the first step to making some allies.

Jordan cautiously shook the other boy's hand.

"Name's Jace. What's yours?"

"I'm Jordan."

Before they could say more, the guards started escorting everyone back to their cells for the rest of the day.

I now have one ally. I wonder if I can break out of here with just him.

Jordan fell asleep on the cold, hard cot.

At around seven the next morning, with the sun was barely up, Jordan was back outside, talking to Jace.

"You're telling me you want to escape?" questioned Jace.

"Yes, if that's possible. You seem to know this place inside and out. If anyone can break out, it's you."

"You've got a point there, Jordan." Jace rubbed his chin in thought. "I could get you out, but I'll need some help from my friends."

"Do what you like, as long as I escape from this horrendous place," Jordan said. *What did I just get myself mixed up in? I don't think I can back down now.*

Laughing, Jace beckoned his friends over and told them about Jordan's idea. Speaking in low voices, they made a plan to bust out that night at midnight, when everyone was fast asleep. According to Jace, most of the guards finished their last patrols at around eleven.

By eleven-thirty, the building was silent. Jordan could've dropped a pin and heard it echo through the whole building. As he waited, his breathing grew uneven, adrenaline coursing through his veins.

At midnight, he heard footsteps in the hallway coming towards his cell. It was Jace and his friends.

"We're going to get you out of here," one of the boys whispered. "Wait right here while Jace gets the key to your cell."

Does my cell have a different lock than the other cells?

In a few moments, Jace came running back with the key in his hand. It took five minutes to figure out the PIN and find where the lock was on the cell door.

"Hold on, just a little longer," Jace said, turning the key in different directions.

The door clicked open.

Jordan burst out of the cell and looked around. Down the hall, he could see glass doors at the building's entrance.

"Yeah, that's the way we're getting out," one of Jace's friends said. "But first we need to disable the sensors and cameras by the door. And that's Jace's expertise."

"Sure is," Jace said. "You guys stay here, and don't get caught!" He ran down the hallway to the control room.

While he was gone, everyone huddled quietly together near Jordan's cell. The less they talked, the less likely it was they'd get caught.

Finally, one of the boys said, "Okay, he's had long enough."

The teenagers ran towards the glass double doors and found that the red camera lights were off and the doors were slightly ajar. Jace stood just outside. The boys walked through the doors and then made sure they were closed securely.

"Great job, Jace," said a boy named Conner. "Let's get out of here before they realize we've escaped."

Jace turned to Jordan. "Now we split up. Don't get caught! If the cops come, we'll get them to follow us." Jace then pulled a black cloth over his lower face.

That I can do. Don't get caught up in the chase.

Jordan nodded and started running. But he didn't get far before he hit an obstacle that he knew he couldn't get through—

Jordan suddenly jolted awake. Remembering he was now again in a holding cell, he tried to slow his heart down.

He stretched this way and that, realizing he was really sweaty. *That memory felt so real.*

A moment later, a cop came to take him to the judge.

Hopefully I won't be in jail forever.

Jordan allowed himself to be led to the courtroom. Standing in front of the judge, he knew he would soon be back at the youth detention center.

The judge droned on about laws, but Jordan wasn't paying attention—he'd already heard that speech. But he snapped back to attention when he heard the judge say, "From what I see, Mr. Thurgood, you're going to be in the detention center for at least two years."

CHAPTER 4

Grace yawned and looked around her, expecting to be in the vehicle with Elijah and his partner. To her shock, she was lying on a gurney outdoors in an alleyway.

She felt pain in her head and several other places. Then she remembered the gunshot and the vehicle skidding out of control.

Where am I? Where's Elijah? Grace started feeling panicked. Checking her shirt, she found that the envelope Elijah had given her was still intact.

"You were out for days," said a man in a white suit, suddenly appearing next to her.

Grace jumped in surprise, not knowing what to say.

"It's all right, Grace," the man said soothingly.

"How do you know my name?" Grace questioned, slowly sitting up. Her head was throbbing.

"A mutual friend of ours told me to look for you and take care of you when you woke up," the man explained.

"So, you know Elijah then?" Grace asked, hope flowing through her.

The man smiled, but didn't say anything.

"Why am I in an alleyway?" Grace questioned, carefully standing up.

"I can see you have many questions. Come, follow me." The man started walking away.

I suppose I better follow him. He seems to know where he's going, and I don't want to be in this alleyway.

Grace followed the strange man.

"You're lucky your injuries weren't worse," the man said, turning to look at Grace again. "Your friend—the guy who saved your life—wasn't so lucky."

"What do you mean?" Grace questioned.

"He's alive, but he has a concussion, a few broken ribs, a broken ankle and arm, and some serious lacerations. I was mighty surprised he could carry you so far from the burning vehicle. Once you were safe, he kept going on his own, but he left a trail of blood behind him."

"Where is he now?"

The man smiled. "Don't worry, he's safe."

As they walked, Grace carefully studied the man. He had brown eyes, exactly like Elijah's. And he looked a lot like Elijah. She wondered why.

After a long and silent walk, the man stopped and started looking closely at a brick wall.

What in the world is he doing? We can't walk through a wall.

After a few tense moments of studying the brick, he pushed on one and it moved in. Grace watched a doorway appear.

This is the weirdest day I've ever had.

"Come, there are people who want to meet you," the man said as he walked through the doorway.

Grace was fearful that either the door would close on her or that she was dreaming. She knew she had to keep following the strange man.

To her surprise, she was standing in a large glass-walled room, and the man was nowhere to be seen. She turned around as if to leave the room, but the doorway was gone.

That's odd. I just walked through it seconds ago.

"You must be Grace," another man said, coming into the glass room.

Grace nodded. "Yes, I am. And you are?"

"Ah yes, where are my manners? I'm Josiah Hale. You can call me either Josiah or Mr. Hale—I'm fine with either." As he spoke, the man smiled warmly.

Josiah was tall and stocky. His brown beard was tinged with red, and his brown hair showed some gray. His eyes were dark green and they had a slight sparkle, as if he'd gotten into mischief and wasn't going to tell anyone what he'd done.

"I can tell you have many questions to ask me. Come, we'll go to my office and I'll explain things."

Grace hesitantly followed Josiah into a long, well-lit corridor. To her surprise, she could see through the floor into the room below. "Is this floor made of glass?" she asked.

"Yes. I must say, you're very observant for your age. This floor is strong enough to hold up to three tons. The room directly below is one of our labs."

"How many labs are in this building?" Grace asked, her

curiosity getting the best of her.

"Well, in this building, there are ten. The building next to this one has twenty labs. These labs all serve different purposes." Josiah smiled at Grace.

"If you don't mind my asking, who owns these buildings?"

"I actually own these buildings, and I'm the boss of this company," Josiah said. "It's not much right now, but once we start expanding the buildings and making the campus bigger, it'll definitely look improved. And we'll be able to do more in our buildings."

Grace nodded, looking down into the lab again, where workers pored over various projects.

Floor that is glass, yet it can hold a lot of weight. This is quite an interesting day, from a strange man leading me through a secret door to walking on unbreakable glass with another strange man who owns strange buildings.

Josiah turned a series of corners before coming to a stop outside a door. Grace could tell the door was made of very strong material, but she didn't know exactly what.

Josiah typed in a password on the keypad next to the door. A sudden hissing sounded and the door opened. He gestured for Grace to enter the room.

She walked into the brightly lit and welcoming room, glancing around the wide office.

He seems to really like art. There are so many statues and paintings I've never seen before. It's clear to me that I need to expand my knowledge in all subjects.

"You like art as well?" Josiah asked, sitting at his desk.

Grace sat down in the chair in front of the desk. "I find most art intriguing. I wasn't really able to further my studies—

especially with art—because of my foster parents. I try to do as much learning as I can in my spare time, which isn't very often."

"Elijah reported to me, as he watched over you, that the parents didn't really treat you very well. That's why you're here, so we can protect you from those who want to hurt you."

"What do you mean, protect me?" Grace asked.

"You already know you're not blood-related to that foster family, but neither is Elijah. From the way you're looking at me, I'm assuming you didn't know that until now. Elijah is a spy who works for me. I tasked him to watch over you and keep you safe from a company that wants not only you, but also your twin. Last I heard, your twin was with the other company, but that was about a year and a half ago. Since then, Elijah hasn't been able to hack into the Adrian Corporation's information."

"So, Elijah has been in my foster family all this time, watching over me and protecting me from some person who wants me?" Grace asked, her head spinning.

Josiah nodded.

"You say I have a twin, but I've never seen them and I haven't ever heard of having one," Grace said.

Josiah sighed. "I know it's a lot of information. Please believe what I say is true. We have an entire file on him. I'll tell you as much as I can about this twin of yours."

He got up from his desk and walked to a filing cabinet in the corner. Muttering to himself, he started flipping through one of the drawers.

What if the information in that file is false? What if Josiah is the person who's hunting me down, but he's trying to act like he's the good guy?

The urge to bolt out of the room was very tempting, but Grace wanted at least some answers.

Josiah finally found the file. He walked back towards his desk and set the file down.

There better be something in that file about who this twin of mine is.

"This file contains all the information we have about your twin," Josiah explained, opening the bulky file.

On the first page, Grace saw a picture of the boy who was allegedly her twin. She studied the photo for a moment, internally debating if what she was seeing were true.

I can kind of see the resemblance. But why was I never told that I had a twin?

Grace looked at the picture for a bit longer. "You're wondering why you never were aware of having a twin," Josiah said, startling Grace.

"Yes," Grace answered, hesitating. *How does he know the question I was about to ask?*

"You and your twin, Jordan, somehow got separated after your parents were murdered. You and your brother are the last of your family line, at least to our knowledge. Your family is definitely full of secrets and mystery.

There's a possibility that I might have other siblings or family members still alive.

"Whoever killed your parents might have also killed the rest of your family," continued Josiah. "It's possible that they weren't able to kill you because that's when the authorities came into the equation. Another possibility is that your parents made sure you were safe before they were murdered. When I became aware of what was going on, I tried to track you both down and keep you safe for as long as I could. I was a close friend to your father. I felt like I owed him to at least watch over you two from a distance. Unfortunately, for the longest time, I was only able to track down Jordan. We lost you once you were put into the foster system. And then the spies who were keeping track of Jordan lost him. Elijah notified me that Jordan was with Dr. Adrian, the owner of Adrian Corporation."

"So, Elijah was already working for this Dr. Adrian?" Grace asked, interrupting Josiah.

"Yes, he reported seeing Jordan a couple weeks after he got hired. Elijah still sort of works for Dr. Adrian. But he reports anything unusual or information he thinks we need to know."

Grace nodded.

"Elijah kept a close eye on Jordan as much as he could," Josiah continued. "It was difficult to get a daily update from Elijah, since he still had to play the role of a soldier and also try not to get caught. Sadly, Elijah wasn't able to learn what Dr. Adrian was going to do with Jordan in time."

"What happened to Jordan?" Grace asked, her voice tight with concern.

"Jordan was used for an awful test experiment, which has killed others. And yet he's still alive and well, considering all that's happened to him in such a short time."

"What do you mean by that?" Grace questioned, leaning forward in her chair.

"Dr. Adrian doesn't like training weak people or having weak people in his corporation. He goes for the people he thinks are the best for specific jobs. If they become weak, he either kills them or turns them into brainless science experiments. If Jordan was weak when Dr. Adrian first picked him up years ago, he could've been killed or worse. But thanks to his powers and whatever else is keeping him going, he's still alive. He was even able to escape Dr. Adrian's grasp for quite a while."

Grace pondered this for a moment. "Why wasn't Jordan in

the foster system, too?"

"Ah, that's what I was going to talk about next. Jordan ran away from the authorities before they were ever able to find him. They suspected that he was killed and only you were left. If you look at the file, you'll see not only his criminal record, but also where he's been. He's still very much alive. He doesn't know anything about us watching him—in fact, he doesn't even know we exist."

"Who else knows about this secret group?" Grace questioned.

"You're the only one," Josiah replied. "The government doesn't know about us yet, which is good. We want to be as inconspicuous as possible. The less people know about us, the better."

"Is this why Elijah never told me where he worked or what he did?"

"Partially," Josiah admitted. "Elijah swore he wouldn't tell a single soul that he was a spy for us. I don't know what he had to do when he got the job at Dr. Adrian's corporation. He doesn't really talk about what he does there, other than whatever information he gives us."

"Is Elijah still alive?"

Josiah nodded his head solemnly. Standing, he led Grace out of his office. As they walked, he spoke in a low voice. "Elijah is still alive, but I don't know for how much longer. His injuries are serious. Burns cover his entire body from when the van exploded. He also has a couple infections that are spreading."

"Why wasn't I hurt worse?" *I hope Elijah will be all right.*

"Elijah was able to throw you out of the vehicle before it flipped over and caught fire. He finally managed to get out and move you as far from the scene as he could. I was surprised by how far he made it before he passed out. I didn't hear from him for a while, so I sent searchers. One of the groups finally found him, but we couldn't find you. The doctors got Elijah stable enough that he was able to tell us your location before he passed out again. I sent my trusted friend to find you, and you know the rest."

Josiah stopped outside a pair of glass doors. They stood silent for a moment. "Well, you should go see Elijah," he said kindly, gesturing at the doors. "Our hospital secretary will lead you to him." Josiah turned and walked back the way they'd come.

I hope he's right. Grace cautiously walked through the doors and stood before the dark- wood desk in the middle of the room, where a woman sat writing in a notebook.

She glanced up at Grace. "How can I help you, young lady?"

"I'm here to see Elijah."

"Oh, yes, you must be Grace. Follow me," the lady said kindly. She got up from the desk and led Grace down a silent hallway.

Glancing into each room she passed, she noticed that the rooms were empty. *I thought there'd be more people in here. It's probably a good sign there aren't.*

"Here you are. Elijah is inside this room."

"Thank you," Grace said. She took a deep breath and walked into the room.

Carefully closing the door behind her, Grace sat down in a chair next to Elijah's bed. Trying not to cry at what she saw, she softly brushed her fingertips against Elijah's hand.

You're going to be okay, Elijah.

Grace silently studied his face. Most of his face was covered in burns, and there were noticeable bruises on what was left of his skin. The rest of his body was covered by the hospital blanket, but Grace could guess what it looked like.

"Excuse me, miss?" a small voice said.

Grace looked up and saw a nurse standing in the doorway. "Yes?"

"Mr. Hale wants to talk to you again. He said it shouldn't take long." Noticing Grace's hesitant look, the nurse added, "I promise Elijah will be okay. If he wakes up while you're gone, I'll let you know."

Grace nodded and stood. The nurse saw her out, and she walked back to Josiah's office.

"Since you have no one to live with other than Elijah," Josiah said once she was seated, "may I introduce someone to you? You don't have to make a decision right now, but I want you to at least think about it."

"I can do that," Grace said.

Josiah looked beyond her towards his office door. She heard the door open and then a man's voice said, "I'm glad you're at least going to think about it."

"Ah, Levi, right on time," Josiah said, smiling.

Grace turned to see who it was. To her surprise, the man looked vaguely familiar. "My name is Levi Greenfield," he said, sitting in the chair next to her.

She nodded and then hesitantly asked, "What do you do here?"

"I'm an undercover spy at the police station," Levi said. "But soon, I'll be moving to the detention center where your brother is being held. As an officer there, I'll be able to keep an eye on him."

Levi smiled at Grace, which Grace returned.

Turning to Josiah, Levi said, "How about Grace and I talk in private? That'll give us a chance to get to know each other, so she can decide if she wants to live with me."

"That's a wonderful idea," Josiah said.

CHAPTER 5

After a lot of thought, Grace finally decided to go with Levi. It wasn't an easy decision, since she wanted to be near Elijah. But both Levi and Josiah persisted that she should go live with Levi.

"I'll let you know if anything changes with Elijah," Josiah said as they stood by Levi's blue car.

"Thank you, Josiah," said Grace. "Thank you for all you've done for me."

Josiah kissed Grace's forehead and gave her a slight hug. When Grace was seated, Levi pulled away from the curb and into the sea of cars.

The car ride was silent as they made their way through the busy city.

After a while, Levi spoke softly. "I know exactly how you feel. I had to go live with other families when I was your age, as well. Getting used to new surroundings and being around people takes time. I'm willing to give you all the time you need."

Finally, someone who somewhat understands me.

Grace looked out the window, watching the world go by in a blur.

An hour later, Levi pulled into the driveway of a pristine-looking home.

Getting out of the car, Grace was surprised at how simple and yet modern the houses looked.

"Do you not like the neighborhood?" Levi questioned.

"Oh no, I really like it. It's better than where I used to live."

Levi opened the garage door and walked in. Grace followed, trying to feel as comfortable as she could.

That night after a long, conversation-filled dinner, Levi broke some news. "Grace, you're going to a public school tomorrow," he said, leaning back in the kitchen chair.

Grace smiled, butterflies fluttering in her chest.

"I know you probably don't want to hear that, but I think it would help you blend in better. Maybe it'll give you a chance to make some friends."

"Thank you, Levi," Grace said, standing up and hugging him.

Levi hugged her back.

I'm really, really excited for tomorrow!

Grace went upstairs to the room Levi had said was hers. As she got ready for bed, she felt full of anticipation. She knew that tomorrow would be the second perfect day of her life.

When she woke early the next morning, she felt as happy as could be. She rolled out of bed and strolled over to her closet. She decided to wear a solid black T-shirt and dark-blue jeans.

As Grace dressed, she heard a clatter of dishes from downstairs. *I better hurry if I want to get to school on time.*

She hurried down the long, winding staircase. But she stopped in her tracks when she overheard Levi talking on the phone.

"What?" she heard Levi say. "You're laying me off?! I've worked with you for five years. I've been loyal to you. I've followed every rule and every order."

Levi listened for a few moments and then sighed. In a voice filled with hurt, he said, "You're laying me off because of budget cuts? You know I've been working alongside you for years, and you're willing to throw all that away? Did you even consider laying off a new hire?"

After a few more words, Levi hung up. Grace entered the kitchen, acting like she hadn't heard anything.

Levi was sitting at the kitchen table, head between his hands. "The sheriff caught onto me," he mumbled. "He has to know I'm a spy. I need to call Josiah."

"Good morning, Levi," Grace said, walking past him to the pantry.

"Good morning, Grace. How did you sleep?"

Grace glanced over at him. "All right."

She grabbed a box of cereal, and Levi stood up and got his bacon omelet from the microwave.

As they sat and started eating, Grace asked, "Levi, are you okay? You seem somewhere else today."

She smiled when Levi gave her a confused look. "Hmm? Oh sorry, Grace. I've been thinking about a friend I haven't seen in a long time."

"How long has it been?" questioned Grace, before taking another bite of her soggy cereal.

"Oh, since high school. We grew distant. I've lost contact with a lot of my friends, unfortunately."

After Grace put her bowl in the sink, she ran upstairs to get her backpack. Turning to her bookshelf, she found the book she'd been looking at last night. *This looks like an interesting book. I'm going to give it a try.*

She carefully put the book in her backpack before running back downstairs. When she nearly bumped into Levi, he asked, "Are you ready to go?"

"Just about," Grace said, running into the kitchen. She grabbed her new phone from the counter and unplugged it from the charger.

After a short drive, Levi pulled into the school's parking lot. "This is your stop," he said, smiling.

Grace smiled back and said goodbye. As Levi drove off, she walked toward the school entrance. She still had a few minutes, so she stood alone outside for a few minutes.

Before long, she noticed a group of three boys looking at her. One was tall and broad-shouldered, with light peach-toned skin and red hair. The next was a little shorter and had black, curly hair and slightly brown skin. The third was short and muscular, with slightly brown skin and straight, black hair.

The boy with the curly black hair walked over to Grace. "Hey, I don't think we've met you before." He shoved his hands into his pockets. "I thought I'd seen every girl in this school, but I've never seen you. My name is Henry. What's yours?"

"It's my first day here. It's really nice to meet you, Henry. My name's Grace."

Henry smiled. "Oh, yeah, the principal told me a new girl was coming. You're in a couple of my classes. Let me show you around."

Grace smiled, but she knew that he'd eventually want to get rid of her and would possibly even bully her. She knew how it went. A really cute, popular guy gets to know you, shows you around, becomes friends with you, but then you're betrayed and have no friends.

I hope I can become your friend. I really need friends.

The school bell rang and everyone started moving towards the doors. Henry stayed right next to Grace. Grace felt kind of bad for him. She didn't want to be a burden to him. He probably didn't want to be around her. From the looks she was already getting, she was being marked as the new kid.

To Grace, everyone looked really popular or well-known. Deep down, she thought she was nothing compared to them.

Henry glanced over and saw that Grace was still following him. When Grace looked at him, he smiled at her.

He stopped in front of a glass wall with double doors. "This is the front office, attendance office, and nurse's office." Grace saw two ladies talking to each other behind a tall cement counter.

When they got to the classroom, Grace sat in an empty desk next to Henry. He didn't seem to notice her. He started throwing paper balls at a guy sitting behind him.

"Hey, Sam," Henry said to the guy. "How'd your marching band practice go? I know you were really nervous about that solo you got."

The boy named Sam stopped making a paper ball. "It went really well. I was so nervous that I'd mess up or completely mix up my notes. You know how Mr. Carlton can be—if you mess up one note, you have to start the song all over."

Henry nodded. "Yeah, Mr. Carlton can be such a stickler sometimes. I remember a girl last year kept messing up and Mr. Carlton yelled at her. She ended up quitting once the season was over."

"I remember that." Sam resumed making the paper ball. "Mr. Carlton can be a pain. He's actually the reason I'm thinking of leaving marching band."

"That's too bad," Henry said. "I think you're really good at trumpet. But your mental health is more important. You shouldn't have to deal with such a mean teacher just to do something you like."

Sam nodded. "I wouldn't quit now, but once we get closer to the end of the season, we'll see."

"You'll have to let me know what you decide to do," Henry said, slapping Sam on the back.

"Thanks, Henry. I'll let you know."

Grace was impressed with how Henry interacted with people. He respectfully listened to what they had to say. He brought up bits of information from previous conversations.

She didn't realize she was still looking at Henry until he tossed something onto her desk. She looked down and saw a little piece of folded, blue paper. Carefully opening it, she read: *I was wondering if you want to hang out with me at lunch. I want to get to know you better, and you can get to know me.*

Grace smiled and nodded to Henry, then she faced forward. She didn't know if he really wanted to be friends or was just trying to be nice. Either way, she was going to sit with him at lunch. Out of the corner of her eye, she saw Henry pump his fist and Sam slap him on the back.

A few moments later, the teacher walked into the classroom, sat down at her desk, and started shuffling books and papers.

Just as the bell rang, five girls walked in. They all wore designer clothing, and they were texting on their phones and laughing, showing each other their phones and laughing even more. The whole class watched as they sat in desks at the back of the room.

Standing, the teacher tried to get everyone's attention, but the girls were still giggling and other students were starting to get rowdy, too. Grace felt really bad for the teacher. Finally, after what seemed like an eternity, the class quieted down.

Grace heard the teacher start calling attendance, but she wasn't paying attention. Henry was playing with his pencil and giving her goofy looks here and there. Suddenly he poked her lightly in the arm and whispered that the teacher had called Grace's name.

Shoot. Now I'm really going to be seen as a weirdo. I didn't mean to zone out.

Blushing slightly, Grace said, "Here."

From the back of the classroom, Grace could hear the five girls snickering at her.

Henry leaned over and whispered, "Don't let them get under your skin. They're always laughing and judging people."

Grace sank into her chair, her face growing hot and red. She didn't want to be the center of attention.

Noticing Grace's embarrassment, Henry grabbed his ears and pulled them outward, puffing up his cheeks and crossing his eyes. Grace couldn't help but chuckle. *He looks like a monkey.*

The teacher was still taking attendance when a crumpled piece of paper hit Grace in the back of the head. She picked it up and read: *Don't get any ideas of crushing on him. He's my boyfriend. Back off, or I'll make the rest of your high school life miserable.*

She turned in her seat, trying to see who'd thrown the note. Unsurprisingly, a couple of the girls glared at Grace.

The teacher finally started class. "All right, students, settle down please. Today, I'm assigning you to write an essay for your future self to read at the end of the school year. I want you all to start brainstorming some ideas so it'll be easier to write your essay later on. I expect you to turn it in one week from today. I also suggest you don't procrastinate on this assignment."

Grace spent the rest of the class period jotting down notes.

The bell rang. Henry got up from his seat, turning to Grace. "I think you also have the next class with me, so we can walk together."

As they walked together towards their history class, Henry asked about the note from the girls.

Grace shook her head and mumbled, "Oh, it's nothing. They were just telling me about the class."

Henry gave Grace an incredulous look, but he didn't push the subject further.

The history teacher called attendance and then began talking about a group history project that would be half their grade.

Henry leaned over to Grace. "Do you want to be partners for the project?"

Grace turned to look at him and whispered back, "I'd love to."

At the end of class, Henry leaned over to her. "See you at

lunch?"

Grace looked over at Henry again. "See you at lunch."

▪▪▪▪▪▪▪▪▪▪▪▪▪▪▪▪▪▪▪

At lunch, Grace started walking over to an empty table. Her eyes were so focused on the table that she didn't notice the leg sticking out in front of her. She just felt a bump on her shin and fell to the ground.

All the food on her tray came crashing down on top of her.

Everyone in the cafeteria started laughing and pointing at her.

As Grace tried to sit up, she saw Henry leave a lunch line and walk straight towards her. When he was just an arm's length from her, he turned to the popular kids' table and glared at them.

Everyone in the room stopped pointing and laughing. Grace noticed there was a flame in Henry's eyes and his muscles were tense.

"What's wrong with you people?" Henry questioned, nearly shouting. His hands were balled into fists.

Why is Henry so angry? I get that he's defending me, but he doesn't need to act like this.

Henry paused for a moment, waiting for his words to sink in. "Don't you all know Grace is new here? If you want to make someone feel welcome here, maybe don't purposely trip them and make their lunch spill all over them. You might as well do it to yourself and post it on the internet for the whole world to laugh at."

Henry looked at every kid in the cafeteria. "I'm sick and

tired of your games."

He helped Grace up and they silently walked to the bathroom. Holding the bathroom door open, Henry watched her as she cleaned up the mess on her clothing.

"You know, you could call your dad to grab a change of clothes for you," he said, looking at Grace in the mirror.

"I know, but I don't want to worry him at the moment."

"Why don't you want him to worry about you?"

"He got fired from his job this morning, and I don't want to stress him more than he already is."

"Well, if you need anything, I'm always—"

Grace interrupted him. "Why are you so nice to me? Nobody my age I've ever known has ever been nice to me, except you."

"Because I know what it's like to be the new kid," Henry said, sighing and leaning against the door frame. "My dad used to be in the military and we've always had to move. So, I really do know what you're going through, starting in a new school with no friends."

"That sounds terrible. I'm sorry, Henry," Grace said, sighing as she continued cleaning herself up. "I haven't had many people be kind to me, so it's hard for me to make friends, trust people, or even have people do things for me, since I've had to do a lot of things on my own."

Henry looked at her with a sad expression. "Your life sounds worse than just moving from place to place. I'm sorry you've had to go through so much crap and deal with people treating you poorly."

A shallow laugh escaped Grace's mouth. "Those crappy experiences have made me stronger. I'm glad I went through them instead of someone else."

Stepping away from the door frame and smiling, Henry said, "How about we go back to lunch? And maybe this time you'll be able to eat."

"Sure," Grace said, smiling back.

Henry and Grace walked down the hallway to the lunchroom. As they passed the popular kids' table, Grace saw from the corner of her eye that the girl named Alexis was glaring at her.

I don't care what she thinks of me. I'm actually making a friend and that's all I care about.

Grace and Henry walked over towards a table where Henry's friends were sitting.

"I was wondering where you guys were," said the pale-skinned boy.

"Ah, calm down, James. I was just helping Grace here," Henry said, smiling.

"So, this is Grace," Henry's other friend said, the one with straight, dark hair.

"I don't think I got your names," Grace said, realizing this as she sat down.

"My name is James," said the pale-skinned boy.

"I'm Theodore," the boy with straight hair said.

"Nice to meet you both," Grace said, smiling at them.

Looks like I've hopefully got two more friends.

Henry's group was eating lunch in silence when Alexis came strolling over with some friends behind her.

"So, you're Grace," Alexis said, sneering, "You're also the one that stole my boyfriend."

"I'm not your boyfriend, Alexis," Henry said, "and I never will be."

"Remember when we kissed on my first day of school? Was

that just a game to you?" Alexis asked, smirking.

What is she talking about?

"I never kissed you, and I've never kissed anybody," Henry said, glaring at Alexis.

"Oh, really?" Alexis smirked.

Henry looked at his friends with a confused expression, then turned to Alexis. "I think you're crazy. I never kissed you, and it's going to stay that way."

Huffing, Alexis started to walk away, but then she turned back. "You'll fall in love with me. Trust me on that."

Once she was gone, Henry turned to his friends. "That was—uh—interesting."

"That was *definitely* interesting," James said, then spooned some mashed potatoes into his mouth.

"Yeah, she's crazy," Grace replied.

James, Henry, and Theo burst out laughing.

"You got that right," Theodore said, still laughing.

The rest of the day seemed to drag on. Grace watched the clock like a hawk, waiting for that glorious moment when the bell would ring, signaling that the school day was over.

The bell finally rang.

Grace heard kids screaming and running down the school's hallways with excitement. She waited until almost all the crowds were gone before leaving the classroom. Henry and his friends were waiting for her outside her classroom, which made Grace extremely happy. She'd been longing to see them after the boring day of learning.

James said, "So, Grace, how do you like this school so far? Besides the fact that Alexis humiliated you in front of everyone in the entire school."

"Well, besides that, school was pretty good. How long have you been going to this school? Grace asked, looking at James and Theodore.

"All of us have been at this school since sixth grade, except Henry came here in seventh," James said. "We all hated it when we first came here, especially Henry. But you just have to hang on. School gets better."

"James, I still hate it," said Henry. "I'm just hanging in there till my parents figure out what they want to do. I might not leave here till we all graduate."

"Anyway, before Henry interrupted me . . ." James said, glancing at Henry with an annoyed expression.

Grace laughed.

"We've all hated this school from the start," continued James. "Just hang with us and we'll make the best of it."

Grace smiled at the guys surrounding her, feeling like she could really trust them. Just as she started gazing at Henry, Alexis and her best friend, Bella, came up and glared at Grace.

The three boys moved in closer around Grace.

"Well, well, well, what do we have here?" said Alexis. "The new girl thinks she can be a popular kid. Now, *that's* funny. Do you really think they care about you? They're just gonna dump you and make you feel bad about yourself."

Standing next to Alexis, Bella laughed.

"Hey, Alexis, why don't you go bully someone else?" Henry said. "Leave Grace alone."

This might get ugly.

"Oh my gosh!" Alexis shrieked. "Did you just talk back to

me, Henry? Nobody ever talks to me like that!"

"Well, I just did. So, goodbye." Henry gave Alexis an icy glare as he led his friends down the hallway.

I didn't do anything to those girls. Why do they hate me so much?

Outside, the four teenagers stopped by a tree near the parking lot. Pacing like a guard, Henry watched the school doors, while the other three sat on the ground and watched Henry.

"What's wrong with Henry?" Grace whispered, looking at Theodore and James.

"Well, he's annoyed with how rude Alexis is being," Theodore said, glancing at the agitated Henry. "She's never acted this bad before."

When Grace got up, Henry stopped pacing. "Are you okay?" she asked.

"No, I'm not okay. These entitled brats shouldn't make people's lives miserable. But somehow they do anyway." As he spoke, Henry's voice got louder. "I'm sick of it—their games, just all of it. Someone should do something about it and not just sit back."

Henry glanced sheepishly at Grace and she looked away, trying not to embarrass him.

"Grace," Henry said. "I'm sorry—about everything. First days of school aren't supposed to be like this."

"I'll admit it's been an exciting one," Grace said, smiling.

"How could you be smiling at a time like this?" Henry asked, trying hard not to smile back.

"Because I feel happy to have actual friends. Friends I can turn to when I need help, when I'm lonely, scared, sad, angry, or even happy. I've never had so much fun until today."

Henry was about to respond when a car honked. The four

teenagers turned and saw Levi's car idling nearby.

"Hey, boys, need a lift?" asked Levi.

"Yeah, we'd appreciate it," Henry said.

After dropping off Henry, James, and Theodore, Levi asked Grace how her first day of school was. "From the way you're looking at me, you hated it, didn't you?" Levi asked, his eyes filled with concern.

Where do I even begin? "School wasn't very good, aside from making three new friends. There's a mean, popular girl who bullied me the whole day."

"I'm sorry it wasn't very good. Just—give it time. I hope your new friends will always have your back. I'm sure there are more kids who're nice like them."

Grace didn't say anything else for the rest of the car ride. *Why would my parents just leave me like this?*

CHAPTER 6

Dr. Adrian stood silently as he watched Grant fumble through the files on his desk. He knew the young man was just pretending to be busy.

"Explain something to me, Grant," Dr. Adrian said coolly, sitting down in the chair in front of Grant's desk.

He noticed the young man swallow and look nervous. *Good. I've caught him off guard. Now he'll be less likely to lie to me.*

"Yes, sir?" Grant asked, looking directly into Dr. Adrian's eyes.

"When were you going to tell me that Jordan is in the youth detention center?"

Grant's face went ghostly pale. "I thought I'd be able to track him down and have him back with us by now." His voice quavered. "But I was wrong. I've been trying my hardest to get him back."

Dr. Adrian held up a hand, silencing Grant. "This is a major setback in my plans, but until we can bring Jordan back, I also want you to keep trying to track the girl."

"I'll need more people if you want me to track Grace and Jordan at the same time."

"I can arrange that," Dr. Adrian said.

Grant was silent for a moment, deep in thought.

"What are you thinking, Grant?" Dr. Adrian questioned.

"Do we have a software developer here?"

"Yes, we do. Several of them, actually. Why do you ask?"

"If we can get a few of these software developers on the project, they can work together to create a better tracking system to find Grace. We are, after all, only using a basic tracking system. If we had something more advanced—"

Dr. Adrian cut in, "We not only find Grace, but also Jordan!"

"Exactly!" Grant said enthusiastically, leaning back in his chair.

"That's a wonderful idea, Grant," Dr. Adrian said. "This is, after all, why you're part of Adrian Corporation."

Grant smiled at his boss, who slightly smiled back.

"I'll let you get back to work," Dr. Adrian said, getting up from the seat.

Grant nodded, and Dr. Adrian exited the room.

Dr. Adrian slowly made his way back to his office.

If Jordan were still here, he could program the technology powerful enough to track down Grace. And he'd feel like he were part of the company, not just a science experiment, even if the experiment had gone right.

A bitter wave of sadness rolled over Dr. Adrian. He had lost one of the smartest people in his company. Jordan felt like a son to him. Jordan was resourceful, confident, fast on his feet, strong, and wise—even if Jordan didn't like what Dr. Adrian had planned.

Dr. Adrian knew Jordan wasn't going to budge and change his mind. He'd shown that on countless occasions. *He thinks he can change the world by being kind to people.* As Dr. Adrian continued his internal dialogue, he angrily entered his office. *You need to show people force to get them to do what you want, show them you mean business.*

To Dr. Adrian, the world was unstable and unable to advance properly. He strongly felt that he needed to be the one who took down the government and rebuilt it to create the better world he envisioned.

Dr. Adrian remembered being told at a young age that if he wanted something, he'd have to work for it. Nobody was going to do it for him.

"I better arrange that meeting before I forget," he muttered to himself, typing his computer password. He clicked on the video-conferencing app and waited.

I hope this conference goes the way I want it to.

Dr. Adrian tapped impatiently on his desk as he listened to the two men in the video conference. This meeting wasn't going anywhere. The two men were arguing over the data sheets he'd sent them days earlier.

Denovan Wallis was bald, fat, and rat-like, while Joseph Roisenberg was skinny, old-aged, and wrinkly. Both men were rich and powerful, but they were so prideful that it made them blind. Dr. Adrian was going to use that to his advantage.

"Excuse me, gentlemen," Dr. Adrian cut in.

Both men stopped talking mid-sentence.

"I can see why you're both concerned about investing in my company. Anybody would be. But you two aren't typical, average men. You're both very wise and know exactly what your companies need. Other companies don't—they take big, unnecessary risks, and they have no idea what their companies need to thrive in society."

Roisenberg sat still, but Wallis was quick to agree with Dr. Adrian. *I knew he'd be quick when there's flattery involved.*

Dr. Adrian pretended to read his own set of data sheets.

"Very well-said words, Mr. Adrian," Roisenberg finally said, his monotone voice cutting through the silence that had settled.

Dr. Adrian dipped his head in thanks.

Wallis said, "I would like to hear more about your corporation."

"Well, the entire reason my corporation exists is because all my teams of scientists, software developers, and so forth want to make this world a better place. Our motto is 'Changing the world one day at a time.' We focus on world problems and try to come up with solutions to fix each specific problem. Solving just one problem could take months, sometimes even years to figure out. But my corporation is dedicated to working the solution until it's perfect."

"There's been a . . . rumor floating around," Mr. Roisenberg said.

"What kind of rumor?" Dr. Adrian asked. *He's going to say the rumor about Jordan.*

Roisenberg and Wallis raised their eyebrows in surprise.

"You mean you don't know?" asked an appalled Mr. Wallis.

"No, I don't. Why don't you two enlighten me?"

"Well, the rumor is that you and your corporation have made a normal human being have powers. That you've tried the experiment countless times and only one person has lived. Is this rumor true?"

"No, the rumor isn't true, merely made up by someone," Dr. Adrian said, waving a hand in the air. *I just hope my other plans haven't leaked.*

Both Roisenberg and Wallis furrowed their eyebrows skeptically, but neither of them pushed the subject any further.

"Could I ask you a question?" Roisenberg asked hesitantly.

"Of course, Mr. Roisenberg," Dr. Adrian said with warmth.

"Is it true that you want to take over the world?"

CHAPTER 7

Jordan paced the small, gloomy cell, trying hard not to listen to the profanities that his fellow jail mates were shouting at him.

I can't lose my cool now. I have to keep my wits and focus or else I may never escape this place.

An officer came patrolling down the hallway. He stopped outside the cell, watching Jordan for a moment. Jordan didn't acknowledge the officer. After what felt like ages, the cop continued down the hallway.

Jordan's cell was bare except for a cot, a toilet and sink in one corner, a single light that flickered ominously, and a small, barred window. He wore an orange jumpsuit with the number 3-0-8-8-2 in black, vinyl lettering on the front pocket.

There was no mirror in the cell, so Jordan had no idea what he looked like now. He ran his fingers through his hair as best he could. Every once in a while, his fingers would encounter a knot and he would attempt to untangle it.

Jordan imagined what one of his jail mates might say if asked about him. "He's a weird dude who just plays with his hair all day. He doesn't talk at all, just quietly observes. Probably doesn't have any friends. Usually just stares off into space. Seems harmless."

He smiled ruefully at the thought. *Wouldn't it be something if someone actually said that? People probably would think that person has gone absolutely crazy.*

"What're you smiling about?" The angry question came from an inmate across the hall.

"Well, I'd tell you," Jordan said, leaning against his wall, "but I don't think it would get through that thick skull of yours."

"What did you just say to me, jackass?" the boy asked, standing up from his bed and moving closer to his cell bars.

Jordan was glad he didn't share a cell with this boy; otherwise, he would have been pounded.

"Speak when you're spoken to," the boy bellowed, banging on metal bars with both fists.

Now would be a great time for an officer to come down the hallway.

Jordan looked up at the ceiling, trying to appear bored.

As if reading Jordan's thoughts, an officer appeared. "Quiet down, number 2-1-6-6-0, or I'll taser you," he said sternly.

The boy instantly stopped hitting the bars, his eyes growing wide with fear.

The cop moved on, leaving the hallway eerily silent.

That's what our identities are now—just numbers, nothing more. If the staff were to learn our names, we'd become more humanized and they'd find it even harder to drag us around in cuffs and be rude to us, so that's why they stick with just our numbers.

■■■■■■■■■■■■■■■■■■

The rest of the day passed by slowly.

I'm so bored. The only way to entertain myself is to either stare at the ceiling or watch the flickering light.

The food Jordan received smelled like rotten fish and tasted like canned dog food, with the same texture. Jordan ate it anyway.

One of the officers gave him a notebook and pencil so he could keep himself occupied. He decided to use it as a journal, written as if someone in the future was going to read it.

March 7th

It's been a week since I came to the detention center. Already more than a dozen criminals have cussed me out, threatened me, and insulted me to my face and behind my back. Little do they know that their words don't affect me. I've heard worse.

When I was in court, I tried to state a case that I'm innocent. But the judge wouldn't listen to me. He claimed that I had no idea what I was talking about.

No matter how much I try, my plans of saving the world from destruction keep getting delayed for one thing or another. I've learned that if I'm patient, my time to start my plans will eventually come.

There's a reason why I lived after the experiment while others have died. There's a reason to my existence. There's a reason why my world has been flipped upside down.

Do I know the answers why? I do not. I cannot even begin thinking of those answers, since they are more in depth and profound than I can even imagine.

I remember years ago when a man I'd known asked me a

question. I can remember it like he asked me just today: "How did you became wise in such a short lifetime?"

I remember not knowing how to answer. But now I know. The answer is so simple. I've gone through so much in just a small part of my life. I've been dealt a terrible life. I could sit and cry about how unfair my life is, but I won't. If I want to make a future for myself, I have to keep swinging back even stronger.

Jordan woke up startled, not knowing where he was for a moment.

He heard the soft snores of other boys in their cells and the occasional jangle of keys from a patrolling officer.

He sank against the wall behind his cot. His eyes felt swollen for some reason and his journal was lying face down on the floor.

How did that get down on the ground?

He leaned over the side of the cot to grab his journal. Opening it, he found that the pages were tearstained, but none of his writing was smudged.

Was I crying last night? I honestly don't remember anything.

Jordan walked to the toilet in his cell. As he peered at his reflection in the water, sure enough, his eyes were still puffy.

At first, Jordan couldn't remember why he had cried last night. But the more he thought about the emotions he'd felt last night, the more it made sense.

He recalled his frustration at being blamed for things he never did.

He remembered feeling helpless. He was stuck here in the

detention center, while Dr. Adrian had free rein to put his plans into action without any interference.

Jordan snapped out of his mini pity party when he heard a metal tray sliding through the slot at the bottom of his cell door. Vertical metal bars ran across the front of the cell, but there was also a solid metal door.

Scooting over to the tray, he studied its contents. The sight of the food turned his stomach sour. There were soggy green beans, a hard piece of bread, brown, squishy-looking apple slices, a cheese stick, and two small pieces of burnt chicken.

The food didn't look appetizing, but Jordan knew he had to eat, anyways. While he was eating, he had a feeling that someone was watching him. Looking up from his tray, he saw the boy across the hall staring at him, the one who'd shouted at him and insulted him yesterday.

"How do you stay calm while everyone else goes crazy in these cells?" the boy finally asked.

He's probably trying to get me to talk so then he can insult me.

Jordan studied the boy. He looked sincere, like he'd asked the question to understand better, not to pick a fight, which the boy would probably loose.

"Well," Jordan finally said, "I do go crazy like everyone else. But what I do about the situation is different."

"So, what do you do about it?" the boy asked, his eyebrows creasing together.

"I like writing down my thoughts and feelings. It helps clear my mind and ease my feelings. It's kind of like therapy—well, free therapy, anyways."

The boy nodded. "That's a great idea. Maybe I'll try it."

Jordan left the boy to his own thoughts.

After a few silent moments, the boy spoke up again. "How

do you not get angry when someone's shouting insults or cussing at you?"

Jordan smiled ruefully. "Yeah, it's hard not to get angry, especially with a temper like mine. I try not to pay much attention to the person and they eventually leave me alone. Try thinking about happy thoughts or even happy memories."

"You're very wise," the boy said. "I've tried to with other prisoners here, but they don't respond. Your advice is actually helpful."

Jordan nodded, knowing what the boy was talking about.

"Did you know," said the boy, "that you're the only person in here who hasn't shouted or thrown something at me?"

Jordan didn't know if he should be surprised or not by that comment. "Really? I'm the only one who's treated you civilly?"

The boy nodded.

"How old are you?" Jordan asked.

"I'll be seventeen in two months," the boy replied. "How old are you?"

"I'm sixteen, and my birthday isn't for a long time," Jordan said.

"Oh wow, I didn't realize we're the same age."

Jordan laughed and so did the boy.

"Well, you have to ask questions to get to know someone," Jordan said, grinning.

"That's true," the boy said, nodding.

"The name's Jordan, by the way."

"That's a nice name. I like it. My name is Braxton."

CHAPTER 8

The lights were all off throughout the entire building and Jordan could hear the deep breathing of sleeping people.

He debated if he should fall asleep or write in the journal. *If I try to fall asleep, I know there'll be nightmares waiting for me. If I write in my journal, I'll fall asleep, anyways. It's a lose-lose situation.*

After much thought, he finally decided that he needed to get at least a couple hours of sleep.

In the dream, fire roared all around him. Jordan could smell burning trees and sizzling tar from the road he was standing on. Smoke blew all around him, and ashes landed in his hair and on his clothes. Jordan paced back and forth, trying to keep himself calm, trying to find a way out of the fiery ring he was trapped in.

Jordan had saved his friends, but he couldn't find a way to save himself. That way typical of him. He was usually the one that got into danger trying to save his friends.

Think. What's the best way to get out of here?

He continued pacing, watching the orange flames rise higher and higher on the taller trees. Amid the fire's roar, he started hearing shouts and popping sounds. His blood turned ice cold, and his heart beat faster in his throat.

Oh, no! Those pops better be from the fire, not from what I think they are.

He heard a few more pops, and then they stopped. If it was gunfire, he hoped it was his friends' guns and not the enemy army. He knew the enemy was well trained. They had the upper hand and a leader, while his friends' leader was trapped in this stupid fire ring with no way of escaping.

Hearing a huge *crack* right above him, Jordan looked up fearfully. His heart started pounding again and adrenaline coursed through him. A large tree was starting to break apart and Jordan was in its path.

Oh, great. My typical luck is going to get me killed.

He tried to move out of the tree's path, but the fire limited his options.

"Jordan!" he heard someone shout from far away. He wondered if he'd misheard because of the loud cracks of trees snapping. But then someone shouted his name again.

Jordan was almost a hundred percent sure he knew who was calling his name. Hearing that voice gave him a sliver of hope that his friends were still alive. Maybe they were trying to find a way to help him escape the fire, or maybe they were just keeping the army at bay long enough for him to get out. Either way, it spurred Jordan into action.

Jordan jolted upright in bed, his breathing labored.

He was slick with sweat.

Pressing his hand against the wall, he found that it was cold to the touch. Shifting in his cot, he leaned his sweaty back against the wall.

These nightmares need to go away. They're getting way too realistic.

Jordan finally found a comfortable position to sit in. He sighed with relief as his body began to cool down.

I need to distract myself so the memories from the dream won't stick in my mind.

He was falling asleep again, and another bad dream started to appear. *No, no, no! I cannot fall asleep!* Growing frustrated, he moved into an uncomfortable position, hoping it would keep him awake.

He thought about his twin. *I wonder what she looks like now. I wonder if she looks like me still.*

He knew he must look much different than he had in the past. For one thing, his blond hair was dyed black. He missed his blond hair—maybe he would let it grow back.

Pulling back one of his jumpsuit sleeves, Jordan looked at his scars. *Battle scars. Maybe once the world is back in order, people will realize all I've done for them.*

He touched his right eyebrow, tracing the scar that started there. It skipped over his eye socket and then continued down to his cheekbone. The scar was still sometimes painful, making him wince when he moved his face a certain way.

Wonderful life I made for myself, huh?

In the dream, orderlies were dragging Jordan from Dr. Adrian's torture room. He'd betrayed Dr. Adrian. At some point during the torture, he'd fallen unconscious and now he felt pain all over his body. All the machines were now off, the bloody tools cleaned up.

As the men escorted Jordan down the hallway, Dr. Adrian walked briskly behind. The men threw him into his cell, where he would recover for the next few days.

Jordan had refused to tell Dr. Adrian the information he'd gathered on Elijah. Jordan knew what Elijah was doing, and he supported Elijah. He swore to protect Elijah's secret and never tell another soul. Jordan had also betrayed Dr. Adrian by refusing to help him take over the world.

Still in the dream, Jordan awoke that evening in his cell. His head hurt. His throat hurt. His entire body throbbed in pain. He tried to sit up, but excruciating pain coursed up from his abdomen. He lay back down on his back. Panting hard, he tried again. Crying out in pain, he eased himself back down again.

Come on, push through the pain. You've had worse done to you before. You can do this.

Jordan attempted to sit upright again.

Twenty minutes later, he achieved standing upright.

Well, now that I'm up, I should find the light switch so I can see what I look like now.

Looking down, he saw burns, bruises, and deep scars covering his body.

He tried to touch some newly burnt flesh, but he grimaced when pain shot up his arm. Taking a deep breath, he touched the burnt flesh again. The pain wasn't as bad the second time.

Looking at his shoulders, he saw that the burns there were more severe than anywhere else on his body. *Those will surely scar up. Nobody will care, though. I'm never going to talk about what he did to me. Right now, I have to heal and get back into shape.*

Jordan woke up from the dream.

CHAPTER 9

Grace strode to school confidently, glad she'd found three true friends who wanted to be friends with her. Levi had been more than thrilled when he found out that she was friends with Henry, Theodore, and James.

Approaching the school, Grace felt a surge of irritation. As if some sort of power were trying to stop her from being happy, Alexis and her friends blocked the front doors.

"Oh look, the new girl's still here. I thought you'd be ashamed to show your face again."

A couple of Alexis's friends snickered at her comment.

Nice to see you, too, Alexis.

Grace pushed past them into the school, smiling to herself when Alexis screamed at her to come back.

▪▪▪▪▪▪▪▪▪▪▪▪▪▪▪▪▪▪▪

When Grace told Henry, Theodore, and James what had happened, they were all shocked. Theodore even began choking on his cracker. As James pounded him on the back, he looked at Grace and said, "You really did that?"

"No, I just made it up to impress you three." Grace rolled her eyes. "Yes, I actually pushed past them and ignored them."

"Aw man, I really wish I was there to see that," Henry said with a grin.

Grace stuck out her tongue playfully and Henry did the same.

"You two are so cute," Theodore commented.

Thanks for ruining the moment, Theo. Grace's face turned pink and Henry threw a piece of roll at Theodore, who caught it in his mouth.

"Do you two like anybody?" Grace asked, trying to change the subject.

James' eyes lit up with happiness, while Theodore slumped in his seat.

"I'm assuming James likes somebody and Theo doesn't?" Henry said.

"More like got rejected," Theo mumbled.

"Who rejected you this time?" Grace asked sympathetically.

"Ellie Adams," Theo said sadly.

"Really? *She* rejected you?" Henry raised his eyebrows in surprise.

"Who is Ellie Adams?" Grace asked.

"She's in Theo's science class," explained Henry. "They've

been friends since seventh grade."

"So, did she not like you, just wanted to be friends, or what?" Grace asked. "You have to give me all the details."

"She sees me as more of an older brother," said Theo. "And she said she likes someone else."

Darn it. Hopefully Theo can find someone else sooner than later.

An awkward silence fell on the small group.

Walking out of her history class, Grace accidentally bumped into Alexis, who didn't appear to be in a good mood.

"Ugh, watch where you're going." Alexis rolled her eyes at Grace.

"I'm sorry, Alexis," Grace said sincerely. "I didn't mean to bump into you."

"Why are you being so nice to me?" Alexis asked, turning around to look at Grace.

"What do you mean?" Grace asked.

"Ever since you got here, I've made your school experience miserable. But you've treated me with nothing but kindness."

Grace sighed. "To be honest, there've been times I've wanted to strangle you or punch you. But I feel like everyone needs second chances."

Alexis looked like she wanted to cry.

Something's not right. "Are you okay, Alexis?" Grace asked.

"I don't know anymore," Alexis said, tears brimming. "Things have been really hard for me lately. My parents are getting divorced, my oldest brother moved out, I'm failing all my classes, and I'm losing all my friends. It's *so* stressful, and I don't know what to do."

That's a lot of stuff on her shoulders. No wonder she acts really mean.

"How close are you to your oldest brother?"

"We're extremely close, practically best friends. We did everything together. But my family's so toxic that he had to get away for his mental health," Alexis said sadly.

"It's good you can still turn to him for help, even if he's not living there with you," Grace replied.

"I suppose." Alexis sniffled.

"Have you tried explaining to your teachers about your family situation or asking for help to get your grades up?" Grace asked.

Alexis shook her head.

No wonder she's failing her classes. "I can help you get your grades up, if you'd like," Grace offered.

"Oh yes, please. I need all the help I can get."

Well, that at least solves one of her problems. "Would you like to hang out with me and my friends?" Grace asked. "That'll at least help you make a couple new friends."

"Sure!" Alexis said happily.

After school, Henry, James, and Theodore were shocked when they saw Alexis walking with Grace towards the tree where they met.

Well, they're surprised all right. The question is, will they be able to speak?

"Would you guys stop staring like that? It's very rude," Grace said jokingly as she sat down on the grass next to Henry.

"Sorry, just trying to get over the shock," Henry said.

Alexis sat down near Theodore and shrugged off her heavy backpack. Theodore looked at her like she was his worst nightmare come to life.

After an awkward silence, James said, "So, uh, everyone . . . what's your favorite holiday?"

Alexis laughed. "Halloween. You not only get free candy, you also get to dress up and scare people. What about you guys?"

"My favorite's Halloween, too," Theodore said.

"That's cool," Alexis responded.

Well, they seem to be hitting it off well. Grace watched Theodore and Alexis grin at each other.

The others took their turns, but Grace noticed that Theodore and Alexis weren't listening.

Leaning towards Grace, James whispered, "Those two are in their own little world right now."

She nodded, smiling. Then, to introduce a new topic, she asked in a loud voice, "James, are you going to say who your crush is now? I've been dying to know since lunch."

Henry, James, and Grace glanced over at Theodore and Alexis, but they remained engrossed in their own conversation.

"Her name's Olivia Foxwood," James said. "She's in my English class, and she's also my next-door neighbor. She's the prettiest girl I've ever seen."

Grace gave two thumbs up. *Just saying her name makes James happy.*

"You two would definitely look cute together," Henry admitted.

Grace didn't say anything, as she didn't yet know Olivia. *I really need to meet more people.*

As Henry and James continued to talk, Grace mostly listened, putting in a comment every once in a while. She often felt more content to listen than to talk.

Looking over at Theodore and Alexis, she felt relieved. Theo was making Alexis feel part of the group. Both looked really relaxed as they talked.

Henry leaned over to Grace. "So, why is Alexis sitting with us?"

"She's had a really hard time lately," Grace said. "I was nice to her this morning and now she's softening up, I guess."

"You're remarkable, you know that?" Henry said.

When Grace got home from school, she sat in the kitchen and thought about everything that had happened. Some of the events were awful, and she really wished they'd never happened. But the good events made up for the bad ones.

I'm lucky to have this life right now. If Elijah had never agreed to become a spy for this Mr. Adrian person, who knows what my life would be like.

Looking out the kitchen window, Grace started playing with her thin, silver necklace. She understood that in order to feel grateful for the good experiences, she had to experience the bad things first.

CHAPTER 10

A short female scientist burst into the room, breathing heavily.

Dr. Adrian looked up from his papers, debating whether he should feel surprised or angry about this sudden entrance. *I guess there must be some sort of news.*

Setting the papers down, he raised an eyebrow. "It looks like you ran all the way to my office."

"That—is—what—I did—sir," the scientist said between breaths.

Dr. Adrian let the woman catch her breath. "This is very important," she finally said. "Carlos sent me to tell you that the plant you requested has been harvested and tested, and it's now ready for your use."

That's good news. I didn't know the tests would be completed so quickly. "I'll go to the lab right away then." Dr. Adrian stood and straightened the front of his suit. "You are dismissed."

Nodding, the short scientist left the room without another word.

That plant will be of great use in days to come.

Dr. Adrian made his way out of his dimly lit, black-and-white office; past his secretary, who on the phone with a client; and out into the stark, white hallway.

The lack of colors usually made people hate this place because it looked like an asylum. Most people feared his building because it wasn't a pleasant place to be in.

As Dr. Adrian walked down the silent hallways towards the labs, he entered notes on his phone about plans he needed to make or finalize. His nose caught the strong scent of chemicals. *I love the fresh scent of hard work late in the afternoon.*

He put his phone in his suit pocket as he walked through the lab's double door.

"Hello, old friend," Dr. Adrian said.

Turning toward him, Carlos smiled. "Hello, Mr. Adrian. I take it my runner told you the exciting news?"

"Yes, she did, once she caught her breath from running."

The young head scientist laughed. "Let's talk in my office."

Dr. Adrian followed Carlos as he began weaving among lab equipment and tables. But then something caught his eye. Stopping, he carefully picked up a jar full of magenta liquid. Reading the label, he was very happy to see that it was another lethal weapon.

Ah yes, poison berry liquid. When injected, the subject will fall into a deep sleep. When they awake, they're easy to brainwash. Too much liquid will cause them to die. Very powerful stuff.

He set the jar back down on the metal table and resumed walking to the scientist's office.

Once Dr. Adrian was seated, Carlos began eagerly talking about the latest weapon. "I'm proud to say that the exotic, toxic plant called Rose Blood has been successfully grown with excellent results. Rose Blood can be consumed straight from the plant or smashed up and put into darts. Either method will have the same effect on the subject."

"And what is that effect?" Dr. Adrian questioned.

"When injected or eaten raw, Rose Blood will paralyze the subject, but also make their body twice as sensitive to touch."

"So, just to make sure I understand, the subject will be paralyzed, but will still feel every little thing that happens to their body?"

"Yes," the scientist said with excitement.

"You've proven this on human subjects?" asked Dr. Adrian.

"Yes. When hit with a Rose Blood dart, the test subject stopped right in their tracks and crashed to the floor."

A dark smile grew on Dr. Adrian's face. "I'll have you work with my weapons designer to create the perfect weapon for shooting Rose Blood darts. Hopefully the design won't take long."

"Sounds good, Mr. Adrian. I won't keep you here any longer. I know you're quite a busy man."

"Thank you, Carlos." Dr. Adrian got up and walked back through the lab. Just as he reached the hallway, the lights went out and an alarm sounded.

CHAPTER 11

What in the world is going on? There are hardly ever power outages in my buildings. And when they do happen, the alarm doesn't go off.

Dr. Adrian groped his way through the darkness, trying to find the door to either the lab or a different room.

Strangely, he couldn't feel any door openings.

A sound of glass shattering drew Dr. Adrian's attention. *Who'd be breaking into this building? How can they see anything in the pitch black?*

He pulled out his phone, tapped the flashlight icon, and shone the light both ways down the hallway. *If I knew where the noise came from, it'd be easier to know which way to go.* Somewhere off to his left, Dr. Adrian heard feet shuffling. He headed down the hallway in that direction. *Better not be any of my guards sneaking off again.*

After a while, he stopped and backed up against a wall, pausing to listen. He turned off his flashlight, surrounding himself in darkness again. Dr. Adrian heard only silence. It made him uneasy. *The alarm got turned off, but where's the lights?*

As if by magic, three flashlight beams momentarily flashed up the hallway in the direction he'd come from. He heard running footsteps.

"Are you sure this is the room?" a female voice whispered.

"The scans say we're in the right place," a male voice replied.

Someone did break into the building. Panic bloomed inside Dr. Adrian. The voices sounded close by, but the hallway echoed, so he wasn't entirely sure. Then he heard a card swipe and saw a little green light.

From where he stood, Dr. Adrian wasn't sure which room the intruders had entered—he just hoped it wasn't the lab.

After a few tense moments, the building lights came back on. Blinking, Dr. Adrian retraced his steps up the hallway.

To his dismay and horror, he saw that they'd entered the lab. Suddenly, the intruders came running back out with canvas bags full of something. He shouted at them to stop, but they shoved past him and ran back the way they'd come.

Everyone who had been on duty at the time of the break-in stood in Dr. Adrian's office. "Did any of you see suspicious people inside or outside the building?" Dr. Adrian questioned.

To his bitter disappointment, nobody but the lab workers had seen anybody or even knew what had happened.

Looking at the lab workers, he asked calmly, "Was anything stolen from the lab?"

The lab workers all looked over to the lead scientist. It was clear they wanted Carlos to speak.

Carlos swallowed hard and said gravely, "Two things were stolen that we know of so far."

"Which were?" Dr. Adrian asked.

"The poison berry liquid and the Rose Blood plants."

This is a major problem for us then.

"Do we know anybody who wants our company to fail?" Dr. Adrian asked the chief guard.

"No one we know of. Most companies have realized by now that they can't beat us."

"Interesting," Dr. Adrian said.

"Could Jordan Thurgood be behind this attack?" the chief guard asked.

Of course somebody would ask if Thurgood was behind this. But I know very well that none of us really think it was him.

Everyone in the room looked at Dr. Adrian.

Dr. Adrian responded, "No, this wasn't Thurgood's doing. He doesn't have the manpower to do it, and besides, he's still locked up in that detention center."

Another guard asked, "Could the government be behind the attack?"

Dr. Adrian laughed. "I highly doubt it. The government has no idea what we've been up to all these years. They wouldn't know unless someone told them. But I doubt anybody did."

Silence filled the room.

Finally, a lab worker asked, "Do we have any security footage to see who did it?"

A guard shook his head. "All the security cameras are either damaged or permanently offline. The only people who can do damage like that are hackers. But the problem is, none of us know any hackers other than Thurgood who can do that much damage."

Dr. Adrian's jaw tightened. After some thought, he came to a reluctant conclusion. "If that's the case," he said slowly, "then there's a new player in this game."

CHAPTER 12

A couple nights later, Jordan sat upright in his cot, sweat coating his entire body. He felt claustrophobic.

Throwing the red, worn-out blanket off, he paced his cell, mulling over what he'd dreamt about, trying to make sense of it.

There must be some sort of group that Dr. Adrian doesn't know about. A group that has hackers experienced enough to fry those security cameras. A group that knows the way around the building.

That's when he remembered a very important detail. *Elijah told me about how he's a spy for this rebel group that Adrian doesn't know exists.*

With sleep now long gone, Jordan jotted down a list.

1. *Figure a way out of the detention center*
2. *Break out*
3. *Find twin and make sure they're safe*
4. *Contact friends*
5. *Gather as many allies as possible*

6. *Slowly end this war*

Outside his cell, the detention building was silent. Juvenile delinquents were asleep, while the officers sat in their small offices or stations.

These silent hours were one of the very few times when Jordan felt relaxed. Nobody was watching him, and he could work in peace.

Jordan wrote a journal entry to record what had been happening.

These silent hours were one of the very few times when Jordan felt relaxed. Nobody was watching him, and he could work in peace.

Jordan wrote a journal entry to record what had been happening.

April 3rd

I overheard a couple of police officers earlier today talking about an officer who recently got fired. The officer was in charge of keeping an eye on me. So, I have a different officer every day now. Or at least until the sheriff comes up with a permanent solution to the problem.

Thinking more and more about the dream I had—feels like it's less of a dream and more of reality.

Elijah told me years ago what his true job was. It slipped my mind until just now.

I have a slight hunch that the break-in I saw in my dream wasn't just some petty company trying to slow down Dr. Adrian, but a secretive rebel group.

Jordan looked at what he'd just written down, wondering if keeping this journal entry was a good idea.

Well, it's a good idea to record all I can. Especially when I have a feeling that my life is just going to become more hectic.

"Couldn't sleep, Jordan?" Braxton asked from across the hallway.

Feeling tired, Jordan looked over at his friend. "Yeah, I had another dream. I felt like I had to write it down before I forget. Why aren't you asleep?"

Braxton shook his head angrily. "My body decided I got enough sleep for the day, so I woke up. That's when I noticed you were up and writing in that notebook."

"A man's got to do what he's got to do," Jordan said with a lopsided grin.

"I suppose," Braxton responded.

"How long do you think it'll take for Mr. Warden here to find a replacement officer for you?" Braxton questioned casually.

"No idea." Jordan shrugged his shoulders. "Could take days, maybe even months."

"I take it this isn't your first time losing an officer?"

"Nope. Not very many people can stick around long enough, since they can't tolerate me," Jordan said, leaning against the concrete wall behind his bed.

Even people who can tolerate me end up leaving.

CHAPTER 13

"Grace, I need to run to work a bit earlier than expected," Levi called from his upstairs bedroom.

Grace was sitting on the living room floor, working on a history assignment. "Okay, do you need to leave right now?" she called up to Levi.

"No, I shouldn't have to leave for about another hour," Levi said as he came down the stairs. "Oh, and Josiah told me to tell you that Elijah is awake and has been asking nonstop questions about you. So, if you'd like, you can go to work with me and see him."

"Okay, sounds good," Grace said calmly as she continued looking over two different papers she was holding up.

When Levi walked into the living room, he stopped abruptly. "Did a hurricane happen in here?" he said jokingly.

Grace looked around at the mess of papers she had made. *Huh, it does kind of look like a hurricane.*

Levi helped Grace pick up her papers. "How about we leave in another hour? That'll give you a chance to finish whatever you're doing. And I need to finish something to give to Josiah."

"Sounds good," Grace said. Levi headed into his office, and she opened her laptop to continue working on her history assignment.

Grace and Levi walked down opposite hallways—Levi to Josiah's office and Grace towards the building's hospital wing.

I wonder how long Elijah's been awake. I know it's been a while since I last came here.

Grace hesitantly entered the reception area. "I'm here to see Elijah Carver," she said to the receptionist.

The receptionist looked up from her computer and scowled at Grace.

Well, she's a ray of sunshine today, isn't she?

"I take it you must be Grace," the receptionist said impatiently. "Elijah is down the hallway to your left. He's in room twenty-seven."

"Thank you," Grace said kindly. She walked down the hallway and stood outside Elijah's room. *I can do this. I can walk into that room and see him.*

Grace knocked on the white door and waited for permission to enter.

That's weird. I don't hear him saying anything. Maybe he's asleep?

Grace was about to walk back down the hallway when Elijah opened the door himself. "I was wondering when you'd come visit me," Elijah said, hobbling back to the bed.

Grace entered the room, closing the door behind her. "I've been busy with school and I didn't know if you were awake yet. I did come by when you were still in a coma."

"I'm just messing with you, Gracie. I didn't wake up until just a week ago, and my doctor wanted to make sure everything was okay before I had visitors come."

"So, how's your recovery going?" Grace asked, sitting on the bed next to Elijah.

Elijah sighed. "My speech and thinking skills are still a little slow. My doctor said it could be a few more weeks before my physical problems are fully healed. But he doesn't entirely know how long it'll take me to fully recover. Could take days, could take months, or even years to get back to how I was before the accident."

Grace nodded. "Well, you certainly sustained a lot of injuries."

"That is true. My doctor told me I was in a coma for three months. That's a lot of time I wasted by being so careless," Elijah said bitterly.

"Do you ever regret saving my life?" Grace asked, looking directly into Elijah's eyes.

Elijah's face became even more serious. "I would do it again and again if I had the chance. I don't regret my decision to save you. I don't regret the time I spent with you. I love you, and I care about you. You really are the only family I have left."

He looks really sincere. "How long do you think you'll be in this hospital room?" Grace asked.

"I think a couple more weeks before I can go back to my apartment," Elijah responded.

"That'll be good," Grace said quietly.

Elijah nodded. "I don't want to be stuck in this room any longer, but I'm not permitted to leave the hospital or continue any mission until I pass all the physical exams."

"Your burns are looking a lot better," Grace said cheerfully. "When I first came to see you, you had burns all over you."

"Yeah, they're healed for the most part. But I have lots of permanent scars."

"Do you know anything about this person named Jordan?" Grace asked casually, hoping the name would ring a bell.

Elijah's eyes lit up. "What'd you like to know about him?"

"You wanted to meet with me, Josiah?" Levi asked as he came through Mr. Hale's office door.

"Yes, I did. Sit down if you'd like, Agent Greenfield," Josiah said.

Levi sat down in a chair across the desk from Josiah. *Must be pretty good news if he's in a cheerful mood.*

"I just heard that a job has opened for a youth detention officer where Jordan's being held," Josiah said.

"That's wonderful! How far away is the center?" Levi asked.

"It's about three hours away from where you currently live," said Josiah.

"What would you like me to do?" Levi questioned. *If he's telling me this, he must want me to either keep an eye on Jordan or break him out.*

"I want you to send a resume to the detention center. Hopefully, you'll get accepted so you can observe Jordan. Later on, I want you to help this kid any way you can or any way he asks. He knows about our rebellion—Elijah told him."

"I can do that," Levi said. "What's the time frame?"

"As long as it takes," Josiah said vaguely. "As long as it takes."

CHAPTER 14

Jordan ate his soggy lunch while he listened to Braxton talk across the hall.

"I overheard two officers this morning talking about this middle-aged man who came in for an interview," Braxton said. "Don't know all the details, but it sounds like he's the only guy qualified for the job."

"Guess what, Braxton," Jordan yelled rudely. He hadn't gotten much sleep and didn't want to be bombarded with information right now. "I really don't care who's going to guard me. I can guarantee the person won't even last a week."

Braxton's smile faded and he fell silent.

Great, now I made him feel bad. If I hadn't opened my mouth, he would still be happy and continue telling me what he heard.

As Jordan watched, Braxton turned his back. Jordan bit his lip. He wasn't mad at Braxton. He was mad and disappointed at himself.

I just made a friend, but of course, I have to ruin the friendship. I do this every time. I start to care about someone, then I mess it up and push them away or they push me away. No wonder people hate me.

He picked himself up off the floor, hoping nobody could see that he was crying.

Jordan curled up in a ball on his bed and silently cried.

Jordan didn't wake up until late morning the next day. The feeling of being alone and helpless was still palpable, and his eyes were still puffy from last night.

He knew Braxton probably didn't want to be his friend anymore.

Ugh, I still feel tired and my head hurts.

"You okay, Jordan?" Braxton whispered from across the hall.

Jordan rolled over to face Braxton. "I'm all right now I know you're still going to speak to me."

"You thought I didn't want to be your friend anymore just because you yelled?" Braxton questioned.

Jordan quickly gave a nod, which made his head hurt even more.

Braxton shook his head. "You'd have to do a *lot* more than yell to lose my friendship."

Jordan slightly smiled.

"I take it your head hurts?" Braxton asked. "You're usually really quiet when your head hurts."

"You know me well. Yeah, my head is killing me right

now," Jordan said, lying back down.

"I know you enough to understand how you act." Braxton smirked. "Lunch should be coming soon, so you'll get a fresh water bottle. That'll help your headache more than our crappy tap water."

Jordan rolled his eyes.

Before long, an officer came down the hallway with a cart full of trays. Stopping at each cell, he wordlessly slid a metal tray under each door.

As the officer neared Jordan's cell, he slowly got up from his cot. Across the hall, Braxton's eyes flashed with concern.

"Thank you," Jordan muttered after his tray came through. The police officer nodded, looked directly at Jordan, and said quietly, "You're welcome."

"You sure you're okay, Jordan?" Braxton asked when the officer was out of hearing.

Jordan nodded as he took a large gulp of water.

Braxton watched Jordan for another moment, then rolled his water bottle towards Jordan's cell.

"Braxton, why are you giving me your water bottle?" Jordan asked as he carefully pulled the bottle though his cell bars.

"You need the water more than I do. I don't have a headache." Braxton shrugged.

Jordan slowly shook his head. "You're nice, you know that? Too nice to be friends with me, and too nice to be stuck in here."

Braxton looked down as if ashamed, his brown hair covering his face.

"Braxton, what's wrong?"

Slightly looking up through his hair, Braxton said, "Remember the first day we . . . encountered each other?"

Jordan remembered Braxton's rudeness. "Yeah, but that

doesn't help me understand why you're ashamed." Stepping up to his cell bars, Jordan looked directly into Braxton's brown eyes.

Braxton sighed. "You say I'm kind, but that's far from true. Jordan, I murdered someone in my family." Braxton's voice rose. "I murdered one of my own family members! I tore my family apart and made everyone I used to love hate me."

Braxton started to sob.

Jordan was too stunned to say anything as he watched Braxton's body shake. *This has been haunting him for a while now. Why didn't he tell me sooner?*

"Braxton, look at me," Jordan finally said.

Braxton looked up.

"Braxton," Jordan whispered.

"Yeah?" Braxton whispered back with Jordan's same intensity.

"We've all done things we're ashamed of. I've murdered people, and I've stolen. My parents were murdered. And I ran away from the scene, leaving my twin sister behind! After that, I wasn't kind to people, even when I was given lots of chances to clean up my act and start a new life. So, out of the two of us, you're the kinder one."

Braxton slightly smiled. "Hmm, I do appear to be the kinder one."

Jordan chuckled, knowing Braxton was right.

"Well, I say we eat before our food gets any colder," Braxton said, looking at his tray.

"Smart idea," Jordan said.

I've been told that I was just a teenager who took too many drugs. But I've never had drugs before and was never aiming to start.

I've had bad luck since I was born. I was told I was in a bad group of kids. Now, that was a funny joke. I never needed to be in a bad group of kids. I was the bad group of kids.

Everyone's wrong when they say I'm the one who murdered my family. I got kidnapped when I was twelve or thirteen. This evil corporation made me who I am now. I'm living in fear, anger, and confusion.

These cops think they can change me. You can't change me. Dr. Adrian broke me down to the point that I can't be fixed again. I learned to not trust anyone, not even the doctors who treated my burns and all my other medical needs. I was really stubborn. Well, that's what everyone tells me. Hell, I don't even trust myself, sometimes. That's until I met two guys who gained my trust and my respect.

Jordan studied what he'd written. *This journal entry certainly sounds interesting. I am not going to change it. Those who read it need to know all the crap I've gone through.*

"A new officer's coming down the hallway," Braxton whispered urgently.

"Must be the person you were talking about the other day," Jordan said calmly, not even looking up from the notebook.

"So that means you have a new officer," Braxton whispered back.

Jordan threw his journal underneath his cot, rested his back against the wall near the cell bars, and tried to act normal.

"Real smooth," Braxton said, rolling his eyes.

"You're just jealous you can't move as fast as I can," Jordan retorted.

"You must be the famous Jordan I've heard so much about," an officer said as he reached Jordan's cell.

Jordan looked away and didn't say anything. *Wouldn't surprise me at all if the other officers said bad things about me to this new officer.*

"Er—anyway, my name is Levi Greenfield. I'm your new officer."

Of course you're my new officer. The poor guy looks like he just got out of training. He's going to want to rethink his decision to become an officer.

Levi let himself into Jordan's cell. "You're definitely a lot quieter than I expected," he said, closing the cell door behind him.

"That's because I don't trust your kind," Jordan said, finally looking up at the officer. *I hope he got my hint to get lost and just leave me alone.*

Jordan glanced across the hallway at Braxton, whose eyebrows were raised.

"Jordan, I realize I may look like your average cop, but I really do want to help you out. I want to help you change your life, so once you're done serving your sentence, you'll be a better person out in the real world."

"You do that." Jordan rolled his eyes. "You'll get tired of me one way or another."

"Jordan, you don't understand. I'm not giving up as easily as the other officers."

That's it! I've had enough of playing the nice guy.

"You don't get it, do you, Officer Greenfield? You don't get that I can't forget and just walk away from what I've seen and done. I can't instantly change my ways and act like a good person. That's not how I work. And I don't care to act like a good person living in a corrupt society."

"Jordan, I'm trying to help you the best I can. For now,

you'll have to just trust me."

Jordan shook his head angrily and said forcefully, "I've heard that one before. And it ended up nearly getting me killed. Why should I trust you?"

Sighing, Levi rubbed the back of his head.

Now he's frustrated with me. Well, I need him to understand that I'm somewhat of a difficult person to work with.

"Jordan, all I'm asking is for you to trust me just this once."

He could tell Levi was serious. *I might as well give him what he's wanting. After that, hopefully he'll give up and I can live my life in peace.*

"I'll trust you this once—and only this once," Jordan finally said after a few tense moments.

Levi smiled and headed for the cell door. "I'll be right back, Jordan. I just need to ask the warden something."

I hope he asks to be transferred to a new prisoner.

As Levi walked down the hallway, Braxton looked at Jordan with wide eyes.

A few minutes later, a couple of cops came into Jordan's cell and cuffed him. As the cops led him away, Jordan smiled slightly at Braxton, and Braxton returned the smile.

At one point, Jordan tripped. *Apparently, I forgot how to walk.* The officers, who were holding his arms, lifted Jordan back onto his feet.

Levi was waiting for Jordan by the front doors of the detention center, and standing next to Levi was the warden.

Oh joy, just the person I wanted to see out of everybody living on this planet. Actually, I'd rather see Adrian or Grant than this guy.

"Mr. Thurgood, I've given Mr. Greenfield permission to take you off the premises for a few hours," the warden said sternly. "Don't give Mr. Greenfield a hard time, or he'll have to sedate you."

There he goes with another speech. "You don't need to threaten me. I already know he'll sedate me if I misbehave."

The warden glared at Jordan. "We've already been over this, Thurgood. You know what I'll do to you if you talk back to me like that."

Levi and Jordan walked to Levi's car. *What is this officer planning to do with me?*

As they drove away, Levi asked, "So, Jordan, how long have you been at the youth detention center?"

"Couple months. I'm sure you've seen my records—this isn't the first detention center I've been in."

"Yeah, I've seen your records." Levi kept both hands on the steering wheel. "It's a bit odd, though—some information seems to be missing."

That's interesting.

"Are you married?" Jordan asked, wanting to change the subject. "Do you have kids?"

"Well, I'm not married, but I do have a foster daughter," Levi said, smiling. "She's about your age. Her parents both died when she was young."

"Really? What's her name?"

"Grace. There's a picture in there." Levi pointed to the center console.

Jordan opened the console and took out the photo. "She's kind of cute."

"I'll tell her a juvenile delinquent likes her," Levi said, laughing.

"How long has she been with you?"

"About two months."

Jordan stared at the photo. *Why does she look so familiar?*

"I bet it was really hard for her to jump into a new life," Jordan said. "I know how she feels. My parents were murdered when I was six or seven. I've been living on my own ever since."

Shit. I let out too much.

"She seems to be handling—wait, did you say your parents were murdered?"

He noticed. I'll just have to be smooth. "Yeah, that's what I said," Jordan murmured, looking away from Levi.

"What's your last name?" asked Levi. "I heard the warden say it, but I need to hear it again."

"Thurgood, why?"

Either this guy has gone brain-dead or he recognizes my last name.

"That's Grace's former last name," Levi said. "And you remind me of her." After a pause, he exclaimed, "You two are twins! That's why you look so alike."

Jordan glanced at Levi like he was crazy. Then he looked out the front window. Their car was approaching an intersection, but Levi wasn't slowing down. They were headed straight for another car stopped at the stoplight.

"Watch out!" Jordan yelled, pointing.

Levi didn't respond. He just stared ahead in a frozen way, like he was having some kind of seizure.

Hampered by his handcuffs, Jordan unbuckled his seatbelt and maneuvered himself so he could stomp his foot on the brake. The car skidded to a stop. Jordan then let up on the brake enough to guide the car to the side of the road. He turned off the ignition.

"Levi, snap out of it!" Jordan shouted at the officer, hitting him on the arm. When Levi still didn't respond, Jordan slapped his face.

I just smacked a police officer. With my luck, that'll cost me more jail time.

Suddenly smiling, Levi turned to Jordan and studied him.

"Hm, very interesting. You're not acting how the other cops warned me you would."

"What're you talking about?" Jordan asked, feeling confused and angry. "I don't want any more blood on my hands." *Maybe I slapped him too hard.*

Levi laughed at Jordan's expression.

Jordan continued to look at Levi like he was high on something or had gone completely insane. *This guy is scaring me. Should I be concerned?*

"That was just a test," Levi finally said. "Would you do nothing, or would you save our lives?"

"You're still a little out of your mind. Can I smack you again?"

Laughing, Levi pointed to his shoulder. "No, but you can punch me here again."

Jordan did so, but not as hard as he could have.

"We better start heading back," Levi said. "I don't want to abuse this privilege."

Levi did a U-turn and headed back to the youth detention center. After parking the car, he turned to Jordan. "I need to tell you something. You cannot tell anybody, understood?"

Jordan nodded.

"I'm part of the rebellion."

CHAPTER 15

After Jordan was back in his cell, Braxton asked from across the hall, "So, why did you act like a jerk to that officer?"

Jordan sighed. "You already know my history with officers, correct?"

"Yes," Braxton replied.

"But that's not the only reason I acted that way," Jordan said, his head hung low.

"What do you mean?" Braxton asked, sitting upright.

"Well, I have a habit of acting rude not only to police officers, but also other people. I don't trust people very easy, so it's a lot harder for me to form relationships."

Braxton fell silent. "It's clear there's lots I don't know about you," he finally said.

"You've only scratched the surface," Jordan replied.

"I have all day and many more days," Braxton said, leaning back against his wall. "Tell me more."

"What do you want to know?" Jordan questioned, moving into a more comfortable position.

"I never knew any of that about you," Braxton whispered to Jordan.

The lights had turned off sometime around ten o'clock, but that hadn't stopped Jordan and Braxton.

Sitting in the dark, Jordan replied, "I don't think anybody knows as much as you do, Braxton."

"That's probably true," Braxton agreed.

"Someone's coming down the hallway," Jordan whispered urgently.

"How do you know?" Braxton whispered back.

"I just do," Jordan whispered as he lay down his cot.

Braxton and Jordan were silent as the person came closer to their cells.

Hopefully we don't get caught.

When a flashlight beam shone into Jordan's cell, he tried not to tense up.

"I know you're awake, Jordan," Levi whispered through the bars.

How does he know I'm awake? And what's he still doing here? I thought he went home.

Jordan rolled over to face Levi.

"I have the night shift all this week, if you're wondering," Levi said. "Just thought I'd tell you, the warden has been keeping a very close eye on you. I'd be more careful what you talk about. The warden already wonders if you're crazy, and you don't want to make it worse."

"I'll do that," Jordan replied.

Nodding, Levi continued down the hallway.

At least he warned me. I'll just have to filter what I say to Braxton in the future.

Jordan tried to fall asleep, but worried thoughts kept running through his head.

CHAPTER 16

In the middle of a business call, Dr. Adrian got a notification on his computer screen.

I wonder what that's about. He stared at the icon as his client continued talking.

When the client finished, Dr. Adrian asked, "Do you have any questions before we end the call?"

"None at the moment. If I think of anything, I'll let you know."

They both hung up. *Now, let's see what this notification is about.* When Dr. Adrian clicked on the icon, a surveillance video popped up. Intently watching it for a moment, he realized who he was looking at.

He's grown up and changed a lot since I last saw him.

Pausing the video, Dr. Adrian zoomed in on Jordan's face.

"Will you have Grant come into my office?" he called to his secretary.

"Yes, sir," his secretary said.

Leaning back in his seat, Dr. Adrian waited for Grant to arrive.

▪▪▪▪▪▪▪▪▪▪▪▪▪▪▪▪▪▪

"You wanted to see me, Mr. Adrian?" Grant asked.

"Have a seat." Dr. Adrian pointed to a chair. "I want to show you something."

As Grant sat down, Dr. Adrian turned his computer screen. "Watch this video," he commanded.

Watching the video again, Dr. Adrian focused on Jordan's body language.

He seems more at peace and perhaps a little happier. I wonder what else has changed about him.

"Where was this video taken?" Grant asked.

"That is the Pocatello, Idaho, juvenile detention center," Dr. Adrian replied.

"Jordan's still in Idaho then?"

Dr. Adrian nodded curtly. *I literally just said that Jordan's in Idaho.*

"What's your plan?" Grant questioned.

He's getting straight to the point instead of beating around the bush like every other time.

"I'm planning on just watching Jordan for the next little while," Dr. Adrian said. "Every time I create a strategy to capture him, he always gets away. Jordan may have a plan up his sleeve. He usually does by now."

"That's a very smart move," conceded Grant. "But how did you get the security-camera footage?"

"I might have a couple guards stationed at that detention center," Dr. Adrian said, grinning wickedly.

"Why does that not surprise me?" Grant said.

"Most of what I do nowadays shouldn't surprise you, Grant," Dr. Adrian said, slightly shaking his head.

Smirking, Grant stood and walked out of Dr. Adrian's office.

Well, that was odd. I didn't dismiss him.

Getting up from his desk, Dr. Adrian walked towards the lab. *I hope Carlos found the formulas to recreate the stolen weapons.*

Reaching the lab, Dr. Adrian swiped his card in the card reader. The green light turned on and he heard a click. Walking into the lab, he saw that nobody was in the room.

I wonder where all the scientists are. None of them should be taking a break right now, at least to my knowledge.

"Is anybody here?" Dr. Adrian called out.

"Oh, hello, my friend," said Carlos, emerging from his office. "I didn't expect to see you here today. Was there some sort of notice I didn't receive?"

"No, no, I just thought since I'm on my break, I might as well see how things are going," Dr. Adrian said.

"Well, that's good, I suppose. Before you pepper me with questions, I'll just tell you right now that the recipes for the two weapons were stolen as well."

"That's what I was afraid of," said Dr. Adrian.

The head scientist nodded knowingly and sympathetically.

"If it makes you feel any better, I've been working night and day to recreate the recipes," said Carlos. "I've almost got them."

"I'm happy to hear that," Dr. Adrian responded.

"Glad to ease your concerns," the head scientist said curtly.

■■■■■■■■■■■■■■■■■■■■

What is Jordan planning? Surely he must want to break out of that detention center.

Dr. Adrian paced his office absentmindedly.

I mean, once he breaks out, I'll need to have somewhat of a plan in place, right? Well, that clearly isn't going to work. If I plan right now, Jordan could do things differently than I expect. No more worrying about it now. Fretting will do more harm than good. I'll create my plan when Jordan breaks out.

Diverting his attention to another pressing matter, Dr. Adrian focused on the break-in, which had happened over a month ago.

Why can't I figure out who broke in? Surely, there would be some evidence left behind. And now the unknown robbers have two secret weapons and the instructions for making both. They'll be able to replicate the weapons and maybe even make them stronger, which could delay or end my efforts to take over the world.

Dr. Adrian's phone started ringing. It was an unknown number, but he answered it anyways.

"Listen to me very carefully," an unfamiliar voice said. "You will never find out who was behind the break-in, no matter how much you search. These people are terribly hard to find. As time goes on, the plans you've made for years will change drastically. Be prepared to fail."

The phone went silent.

CHAPTER 17

Grace woke up early the next day, but was not in a huge hurry to get out of bed.

It was a bright and beautiful Saturday morning. With nothing requiring her attention, Grace was going to enjoy her Saturday to its fullest.

After about an hour of watching TV, Grace finally climbed out of bed.

Levi must not be up yet if the house is still silent.

Grace brushed out her brown hair and put it up into a ponytail. She then picked out a white t-shirt, black ripped jeans, and a gold necklace to complete the look.

That looks pretty nice.

Grace studied herself in the full-length mirror.

The house was still quiet. She carefully walked down the stairs and into the kitchen. Everything looked just the way it had the day before, except for a small white note on the counter.

She walked over and opened the note. *Went to work early this morning. Won't be back until this afternoon. Don't get into any trouble while I'm gone.* It was signed by Levi.

Laughing to herself, Grace refolded the note. *I wonder if Henry's up. He should be, since it's now nine in the morning.*

Grace grabbed her phone that was sitting on the counter. Henry's phone rang a couple times before he answered.

"Hey, Henry, are you busy?" asked Grace.

"No, I just woke up," Henry said.

Trying not to laugh, Grace said, "Listen, if you could come to my house in about twenty minutes, that'd be great."

"Okay. What time do you—"

Grace hung up on him.

Ten minutes later, Grace was finishing a piece of toast when she saw Henry walk up the driveway.

"I'm here," he called, opening the front door.

"In the kitchen," Grace called back.

Henry appeared in the kitchen a few moments later. He'd left his shoes next to the front door.

"I see you just rolled out of bed," Grace said jokingly.

Henry laughed. "I was up late finishing an essay. I went to bed at probably three in the morning, and then you called me at nine. Cut me some slack."

"I'll let it go—this time," Grace said with a small smile.

He followed her into the living room. Settling on the couch, they both started scrolling on their phones.

"Did you see the video of the guy stealing a car near here?"

Henry asked. "I guess it happened a few weeks ago."

Grace watched the video on Henry's phone. It was grainy, as if taken at night. The footage showed a young man breaking into a car in a shopping center's nearly empty parking lot and then hotwiring the car. When the video zoomed in, the person's face was pixelated, but Grace could tell it was Jordan.

Not sure she could trust Henry, Grace asked, "Henry, who is this person?"

I hope he doesn't see that I'm lying right to his face. I already know a lot about Jordan, but I don't want Henry to know that.

"Let's try this link," said Henry.

I hope we find out something about Jordan that I didn't know before.

When Henry clicked the link below the video, numerous articles popped up.

"Wow! Someone must be a fan of this person," Grace exclaimed as Henry scrolled.

Henry finally tapped on one of the articles and a picture of Jordan came up.

That's him all right. He's changed a little compared to the picture in his file.

"Henry, I know him!" exclaimed Grace, deciding to trust her friend.

Henry looked at Grace quizzically.

"I know it seems crazy, but I've seen him before. It's hard to explain."

"I believe you, Grace," said Henry, still looking puzzled. "I don't think you're crazy. This Jordan person actually looks a bit like you. Could he be your cousin or maybe even your sibling?"

"I don't remember Levi talking to me about having a sibling. But I surely know him."

That's a lie. I know all that Levi knows about Jordan. And Levi promised me that if he learns more, he'll tell me.

■■■■■■■■■■■■■■■■■■

When Levi came home around noon, Henry was just leaving to get ready for his soccer game.

"Sorry, Levi," Henry said as he slipped on his shoes. "I should've told you I was coming over."

"It's fine, Henry," said Levi. "I'm glad Grace had some company."

As soon as Henry left, Grace asked, "Dad, do you know any more information about Jordan?"

Levi sat down on the couch. "I could pull up his youth detention file. That might have some info we haven't gathered yet."

"Thanks, Dad," Grace said.

"Of course, Grace. I'd do anything for you—within reason, of course." Levi gave her a slight smile.

Grace smiled back. "How do you know Henry? I didn't introduce him very well when you picked us up from school."

"His dad and I are good friends. We served in the military together. Henry knows me because I often hang out with his dad."

"That's cool. I didn't know that."

With a smile still in his voice, Levi said, "I have to leave in about an hour, but I should be back by tonight."

"Okay, sounds good. Where are you going?" Grace asked.

"On a date with someone I went to high school with," Levi answered.

It's about time he went out on a date.

Grace smiled at Levi before diverting her attention to her phone.

After Levi left, Grace wondered if Henry, Theo, and James could come over. *I think Henry said his soccer game was over at three.*

She went onto the group chat. *Anybody free to come over and hang out?*

Theo responded instantly: *I'm down. Coming over right now.*

A few minutes later, James responded: *Just coming home from soccer game. Henry and I will be over in a couple minutes.*

Someone knocked. Grace got up from the couch. When she opened the front door, Theo was standing there.

"I'm glad you asked us over," Theo said, walking into the house. "I was so bored that I was about to do yardwork."

Grace laughed. "Well, you're not the only one who's bored. I've just been home all day."

Theo was about to say something when the front door opened and James and Henry walked in.

"Hello again," Henry said, taking off his soccer cleats.

The four teenagers went into the living room to watch a movie and enjoy each other's company.

CHAPTER 18

"I got permission from the warden to let you use the computers," Levi said to Jordan, slightly out of breath from the long journey to Jordan's cell. "But only if I watch you very carefully." Levi began handing Jordan items through the cell bars. "Here's money, clothes, water, a backpack, a flashlight, and a small pistol."

"How did you get all this in here?" Jordan asked.

Levi smiled. "That's for me to know and you never to find out."

Jordan put the pistol in the waistband of his pants, then carefully stowed the rest of the supplies under the bed. *I missed the feeling of a gun, the cold metal against my skin.*

Levi looked around, not saying anything for several moments.

Is he being followed or watched?

Leaning forward, Levi whispered, "Actually, I went around the scanners, so they wouldn't pick up all this stuff. I also rewired the surveillance cameras, so the guards are just watching the same video loop over and over again.

I didn't know he had capabilities like that.

"That makes sense," Jordan said. "When do I get to use a computer?"

With a slight smile, Levi said, "How about right now?"

■■■■■■■■■■■■■■■■■■

Jordan didn't feel like sitting in the computer chair, so he stayed standing. The news was full of articles about him, but he didn't want to look at them.

Focus, Jordan. You don't know how much more time you have on the computer. An opportunity like this won't come up again anytime soon.

Going back to the search bar, Jordan looked up news articles about Dr. Adrian, trying to see what had been going on. As he scanned dozens of articles, he stopped when one headline caught his attention: *Adrian Corporation Building Broken Into by Unknown Criminals.*

"I'd like to know how they got in," Jordan muttered under his breath.

Clicking on the article, he quickly scanned through it, including photos of the crime scene. *The criminals did a really good job of not leaving any evidence behind. There's only one person I know who could pull off something like this.*

Next, Jordan opened Google Maps and identified a few routes he could take once he escaped this place. Then he cleared the browser history.

"Did you do everything you needed?" Levi questioned when

Jordan walked up to him.

"Yes, I did," Jordan replied.

Levi nodded once. "And you have the pistol?"

Jordan pulled up his shirt slightly. Levi stared at the pistol for a moment, then whispered in Jordan's ear, "There's only a couple bullets left in that magazine. I'll give you more ammo tomorrow."

Smiling, Jordan whispered back, "Sounds good. I better get back to my cell before the warden gets suspicious."

"Come on, troublemaker," Levi said sternly.

Jordan watched Braxton pace his cell nervously.

"You know I'd take you with me if I could, Braxton," Jordan said, putting his journal away.

"Then take me with you," insisted Braxton.

Shaking his head, Jordan said, "We've gone over this multiple times. It would look more suspicious if two of us escaped at the same time."

Braxton looked at Jordan with pleading eyes.

Gah, he has to stop giving me those eyes or I'll end up doing whatever he wants. He knows I have a soft spot for him.

"Please?" Braxton begged.

"You know how to twist my arm, don't you," Jordan said, trying to look stern.

Smirking, Braxton said, "Yeah. It's hard, but I know you'll

eventually crack."

He's always very determined to get what he wants.

"So?" Braxton urged.

Jordan sighed. "I'll talk to Levi and see what we can do."

Braxton pumped his fist in the air, making Jordan smile. "I can't make any promises though," he said, growing serious. "Levi's already risking his job to help break me out."

"All right," Braxton answered.

"Better get some sleep. Who knows what tomorrow will bring," Jordan said, climbing into his cot and falling asleep within seconds.

"You both want to break out?" Levi questioned incredulously.

"That's correct, Officer Greenfield," Braxton replied confidently.

"Braxton, you can just call me Levi. You don't have to be so formal."

"Okay, Officer Greenfield," said Braxton.

Jordan tried to hide his smile.

"I think we should have Braxton escape first," said Levi. "That way, if the warden decides to give anybody a punishment, it'll be you, Jordan."

"Why do you want Jordan to take the punishment?" questioned Braxton, eyebrow raised in concern.

"I'm used to being punished for things I either did or didn't do, and I'm also used to pain," responded Jordan. "Guess you could say I have a really high pain tolerance."

Braxton's brow furrowed.

"Care to tell Braxton more about this?" Levi asked.

"I think both of you need to know something," Jordan said, sitting up straighter.

"Go ahead," Levi and Braxton said together.

Jordan sat for a moment before speaking. "You both already know a lot about my background, but I'll tell you what I kept secret. When I didn't listen or do what Dr. Adrian said, he'd make an example of me in front of his guards. He enjoyed seeing the pain in his soldiers' eyes as they watched me nearly die."

"So now you're immune to pain," Levi finished for him.

"Not entirely immune, but close," Jordan said.

"I'm willing to escape first," Braxton said.

That's a relief. I can't let a friend take the punishment for something I did.

"You may want these, then." Kneeling next to his bed, Jordan retrieved the items that Levi had given him and handed them back to Levi through the bars.

When Jordan started to pull the pistol from his waistband, Levi spoke up. "I have another pistol for Braxton, if you want to keep that one."

"It's all right, Levi. There's a chance the warden could find it on me if he does a random search."

Nodding, Levi accepted the pistol and took the gear over to Braxton.

"When will I be escaping?" Braxton questioned as he put the pistol in his own waistband.

"Tomorrow night, five minutes after midnight," Jordan said. "That's when the other officers will still be in their offices and nobody's doing patrols." He looked to Levi for confirmation.

"What Jordan says is correct. I have a timer on the cameras so they won't pick up on you escaping the building."

Levi walked away without another word.

He spent more time talking to us than he probably wanted to.

"Jordan?" Braxton asked.

"Yeah?"

"Are you okay?"

Jordan was silent for a moment, trying to come up with a response. "I'm all right, just concerned about you."

"Why?" Braxton asked.

"If something bad happened to you, I don't think I could get over it. So many things could happen to you."

Braxton looked directly at Jordan. "I know having me leave first was a hard decision for you. But deep down, you know that's what needs to happen. It'll be the same for me. Whatever happens to me, good or bad, it'll be because I had to make those tough decisions. I know I'll be able to get through this one way or another."

Deep down, Jordan knew Braxton was right.

Moments of silence passed as the two boys were deep in their thoughts.

"We should probably go to bed," Braxton finally said.

Jordan laid his head on the pillow and looking up at the concrete ceiling.

CHAPTER 19

"Look at those scars and burn marks," said Henry. "Do you think he was in an accident?"

Grace and Henry were looking at Jordan's picture. It lay on the kitchen counter along with the rest of Jordan's file, which Levi had stolen from the warden.

"Levi said he wasn't in an accident," said Grace. "He said Jordan claimed he'd been tortured. That's why Levi is working with him. He's the only one who can handle Jordan. He's the only one Jordan cooperates with."

"How long has Levi been working there?" asked Henry, continuing to study the picture.

"About three months now. Levi tells me Jordan's doing better. His health has improved since that picture was taken."

Levi came in from his office with a stack of papers.

"How's Jordan today?" Grace asked.

"He's doing all right, just going through a rough patch a

the moment," replied Levi.

"Well, the good part is that he's doing better than last time I asked," Grace said, smiling slightly.

Levi nodded. "That is the good part."

"What's the bad part?" she questioned.

"One of the prisoners escaped last night and is running loose."

Levi had told Grace yesterday that he would be helping two juvenile delinquents escape. "Was it during your shift?" Grace asked, concerned for her dad's job.

"No, a couple hours after. So, the warden isn't blaming me or questioning me."

"That's good to hear," said Grace. Changing the subject, she asked, "Can Henry stay over for dinner?"

"Sure, but I have to leave for work soon," Levi replied as he went up the staircase.

"Thanks, Dad," Grace called after him.

"Do you think this information is reliable?" Henry asked, laying his hand on Jordan's file.

"I think it's accurate," Grace responded.

"Why do you think that?" Henry questioned, one eyebrow raised.

"Because the government wrote it, and it's based on their research," Grace observed.

"How do you know it's written by the government?" Henry interrogated.

"Because of this stamped government seal," Grace said, pointing.

Henry looked surprised as he studied the seal. "Oh, you're right. So, how would you react if Jordan was your brother or another family member?"

Grace thought hard for a moment. "I would be a little surprised if he's a family member, that's for sure. But I would still accept him, no matter what he's done or what his past was like."

"That's very wise, Grace. I wish more people were like you. The world would be a better place."

"Want to watch a movie or something?" Grace offered, changing the subject.

"That would be a good distraction after seeing that file," said Henry. "I feel really bad for this poor guy. He's had an awful life."

A couple hours later, Henry left for home.

"I'll see you Monday," Grace said, waving goodbye. *I hate being home alone. Nobody to talk to, nobody to help pass the time, and I don't feel safe.*

Grace picked up Jordan's file and sat on the couch to read some more. She paused at a highlighted portion about Jordan claiming he'd been tortured. *I wonder why they didn't send someone to investigate. Dr. Adrian could be torturing people, but nobody would know.*

At about eleven-thirty that night, Grace rubbed her eyes. She had read the file cover to cover, but she still wasn't fully satisfied. *There's something odd about all this. I wish I could ask Jordan himself if this information is true. If it isn't, he could tell me what really happened.*

Getting up from the couch, she slowly made her way throughout the house, turning off the lights except for the light above the kitchen sink. When Levi worked late, she left that one on so he could see when he got home.

I wonder what time he'll be home tonight. Probably not till tomorrow morning.

A creaking sound came from upstairs. Grace turned the kitchen lights back on. When she heard another creak, her heartbeat quickened. *There must be someone in this house. Sometimes the floor in the upstairs hallway creaks like that.*

Another creak.

Gathering her courage, Grace grabbed the biggest kitchen knife. She pulled up her dad's number on her phone so it would be ready if she needed to call him, then slipped her phone into her back pocket. Leaving the kitchen, she crept around the main floor, looking for any signs of an intruder. But she saw nothing out of the ordinary.

Then she heard another creak.

I have to go up there and look before I call Dad.

Taking a deep breath, she slowly made her way up the winding staircase.

CHAPTER 20

"How long have you had those burns?" Levi asked, pointing at the scars on Jordan's arms.

It was hot in the detention center because the air conditioner was broken. Jordan had rolled up his sleeves as he was going through the backpack Levi had brought him. He was breaking out tonight.

"These are recent," Jordan said, looking down at his bare forearms.

"I could find you some kind of long-sleeve T-shirt so you won't be self-conscious," Levi offered.

"As nice as that sounds, it's going to be warm tonight," Jordan responded. "I don't want to sweat a lot while I'm trying to escape. The scars don't bother me that much."

Nodding, Levi said, "All right, there's a short-sleeve T-shirt in the backpack."

"Thanks, Levi, for all you've done for Braxton and me,"

Jordan said.

"Of course, Jordan. It wasn't fair for you to be blamed for something you didn't do."

"One day, everyone in the world will know what truly happened. One day, they'll know the truth. Nobody can be in the darkness forever."

"Those are the words of a fighter," Levi said.

Slightly smiling, Jordan asked, "So you think I'm a fighter now?"

"I always knew you were, even before I met you. There's more to you than what meets the eye."

Jordan didn't say anything.

"Do you remember the plan?" Levi asked, growing serious.

"Yes, I remember."

"I hope so, or you'll be fighting your way out of here. I'll see you tonight before you leave," Levi whispered before walking away.

Jordan checked all his gear one more time, then slipped on the clothes from the backpack.

I hope everything goes according to plan, because I really don't want to fight my way out of here.

Slipping his pistol into the waistband of his jeans, he took a moment to adjust the piece, making it less noticeable.

At around dusk, Jordan sat on his cot, waiting for Levi to come back.

When Levi finally arrived, Jordan's heart rate quickened and adrenaline pulsed through him.

"Are you ready?" Levi questioned, slipping the cell key through the bars.

"As ready as I'll ever be," Jordan said, taking the key from Levi.

"One last thing, here's my phone number if you ever need to call me for any reason." Levi slipped Jordan a business card.

Stashing the card inside the backpack, Jordan said, "Thanks, Levi, I promise I'll make this up to you."

"It's all right, Jordan. You staying alive and keeping out of trouble will be payment enough."

Jordan smiled. "I cannot guarantee I'll stay out of trouble."

"Oh, I know that very well." Levi smiled back. "Just remember what I said when you're thinking about doing something erratic." Levi started moving away from the cell. "Farewell, Jordan. I hope to see you outside this cell at some point in the future."

"I'm sure you will," Jordan said, giving Levi a slight nod.

As Levi walked down the hallway, Jordan sat on the floor and wrote in his journal. When he was done, he pulled out an article he'd printed titled "The Fight for Her Life," by Kai Goodwin.

> *Thirty-four-year-old Levi Greenfield has lived in Boise, Idaho, all his life and still resides there today. He recently adopted a girl named Grace, who is sixteen years old. Grace was in several foster families before finding a permanent home.*
>
> *While living with a previous foster family, Grace was kidnapped by two unknown people, who police are still searching for. Her foster family did not attempt to find her, showing that they never cared about her to begin with.*
>
> *Grace recalls, "My foster family always made sure I knew they didn't want me and I didn't belong there. They didn't*

treat me the best, but I was used to that, thanks to a couple of previous foster families I've been in. I never remembered what being loved felt like, because there was hardly a time I did feel loved."

This just shows that there are children out there who don't know what love is, only pain, sadness, and betrayal. The good news is that both Levi and Grace are now happy. They needed each other more than they'll probably admit.

Levi got hired a few weeks ago at the youth detention center. He is currently working with a difficult juvenile delinquent named Jordan Thurgood. Levi stated that his colleagues thought nobody could get near Thurgood without getting hurt one way or another, but Levi has proved this to be false. To his great astonishment, he has now worked with Jordan for three months.

Jordan felt bad for his twin sister. He knew she deserved so much better than what life had given her so far. But he also knew that Levi was the perfect father figure for her.

Jordan heard people coming down the hallway.

"How long does the tracker last?" the warden's voice inquired.

A male voice replied, "Once it's in his bloodstream, it'll last for about a year, maybe more."

Fear hit Jordan like he had just run into a concrete wall. *That's not good if they're going to be able to track me. It'll be a lot harder to escape. And they'll be able to find where I am, so I could be dragged back here.*

"That's excellent news!" the warden exclaimed. "We don't want any more juvenile delinquents escaping."

The warden and the other voice laughed.

Jordan heard additional footsteps approaching. "Ah, Warden,
there you are," Levi's voice called out.

"What can we help you with, Officer Greenfield?" the warden asked.

"Jordan already received a tracker just yesterday," Levi answered. "Another doctor came and did it while I was on duty."

"Is that so?" questioned the warden, his voice sounding incredulous.

"Yes," Levi said firmly.

"All right, if you say so, Officer Greenfield," the warden said. "I'm trusting you. Sorry to waste your time, Doctor."

"No problem," the doctor said.

Hearing the three men walk back the way they'd come, Jordan sighed with relief. Levi had just saved him from being tracked. *I really do owe him.*

It was now past midnight. The detention center had remained quiet since the close call with the warden and the doctor two hours earlier.

With Levi no longer at work and the on-duty officers sitting in their offices, Jordan knew it was time to leave. Soundlessly, he crouched down to grab the backpack from under his cot.

Don't make a sound, don't make a sound. Jordan carefully opened his cell door. Thankfully, it didn't creak like usual.

That was the easy part. Now I have to make it past the other cells and the offices.

Walking on the balls of his feet, Jordan slowly made his way through the hallway as silently as he could.

As he neared the offices, he felt cold sweat running down his
back.

Hopefully nobody decides to take a stroll outside their office right now.

Jordan was now at the entrance. Levi had told him the code to unlock the front doors. Slightly astonished that he hadn't been caught yet, he punched in the code. The keypad light turned green.

Everything seemed calm, still, and quiet.

How has nobody seen me by now? Surely someone would've raised an alarm or something.

Jordan was afraid of silence. He knew that silence was never good. But he didn't have time to worry about that. He needed to get out of there fast.

Opening one of the glass doors, he slid his body through without any problem. He carefully closed the door behind him, turning around to make sure it closed. The keypad light turned red again.

I cannot believe that after months of waiting, I'm now free! I haven't felt like this in such a long time.

A slight breeze went through Jordan's long, matted hair.

Let's see what kind of transportation I can find, so I can get to my next destination.

Jordan walked briskly away from the building.

■■■■■■■■■■■■■■■■■

After a few minutes of searching, Jordan saw a motorcycle in a nearby parking lot. Carefully and stealthily, he ran towards it.

There wasn't a key in the ignition, so he decided to see if he could remember how to start it using his knife.

Where is it? Jordan went through his bag, searching for the pocketknife Levi had given him. After a couple moments of struggling, he finally found it at the bottom of the bag.

It took him a few tries, but Jordan finally started the motorcycle.

I wonder if Levi left this motorcycle for me. Why would Levi continue to help me and expect nothing in return?

Dawn was coming and all the guards would be up soon. Revving the motorcycle, Jordan rode away.

CHAPTER 21

"Why didn't you knock on the door like a normal person?" Levi asked Braxton again. Braxton was sitting on the couch, looking down at the ground.

Two nights ago, Braxton had scared Grace when he entered the house through an unlocked bedroom window.

Levi was still upset about that.

"I thought nobody was home," Braxton said defensively.

"Even if someone *wasn't* home," Levi said sternly, "that doesn't mean you should climb through a window."

"Well, now we know your daughter is pretty good with a knife. She almost cut me."

Sighing, Levi rubbed the back of his head, feeling twenty years older. "Braxton, stop trying to change the subject."

"I didn't mean to scare her," Braxton answered.

"I know, but if you're going to live here, I need to teach you *not* to climb through random people's windows in the middle of the night."

"When's Jordan supposed to be coming here?" Braxton asked.

"Well, it depends on if everything went according to plan. If nothing went wrong, he should arrive in a day or two, if he's traveling by night. If something did go wrong, either it'll take him longer or he's still stuck inside the detention center."

Braxton nodded.

"You'd been sort of sad all week," Levi said. "Are you all right?"

"Yeah, I'm all right. Just not used to being back in society, I guess."

"In what way?" Levi asked gently.

"I just feel like I don't belong anywhere." Braxton shook his head slightly. "Society has changed since the last time I was out and about. I just look like a weird outcast."

There might be more than what he's telling me.

"There's also the fact that . . ." Braxton started but then paused.

"The fact that what?" asked Levi, raising an eyebrow.

"I basically have no family, since my biological family disowned me when I went to jail," Braxton said sadly.

I could bring him in permanently. He has no family and no home. This house has plenty of room.

"Maybe you could be a member of this family," Levi said. "I'll see if I can foster you long term or even adopt you."

"I would love that very much," Braxton said, smiling for the first time in the past couple days.

It's nice to see him smiling again.

"I was hoping you'd say that," Levi said, lightly slapping Braxton on the back.

Grace walked into the living room. "Weren't you supposed to work today, Dad?" She gave Braxton a slight nod.

"I have another night shift tonight," Levi responded.

"I hope there aren't going to be anymore . . . unknown people randomly showing up in the middle of the night," Grace said, trying to look serious.

"I don't think there will be," Levi said confidently.

"Jordan is supposed to be coming, right?" Grace asked.

"That's the plan, if he doesn't change his mind," Levi said. "But he knows to call me first so I can meet him somewhere, instead of just showing up when I'm not around."

"Well, that would've been nice to know, instead of getting knifed," Braxton complained.

"Where's the fun in that?" Grace asked with a smirk.

Braxton laughed at Grace's comment.

"Grace," Levi warned.

"I don't know how he'll handle three teenagers at once, if Jordan comes," Grace remarked, smiling at Braxton.

"You two aren't funny," Levi commented.

"Well, we both think we are," Braxton said.

"I'm going back to my office. You two can continue being . . . funny," Levi said, getting up from the couch.

■■■■■■■■■■■■■■■■■■

"What's wrong with Levi?" Braxton asked as he and Grace walked outside. "He seems tired."

"He's just really stressed because of work," Grace explained.

"What's going on at the detention center?" questioned Braxton.

"Well, since you and Jordan broke out, the warden's making all the officers work double shifts and get interrogated. Dad has to work the late-night shift all the way to the afternoon shift. That's a long time without any sleep."

"Oh, that makes sense, I suppose," Braxton replied, rubbing the bandage on his arm.

"I wouldn't worry," Grace said soothingly, reaching up to put a hand on Braxton's shoulder. He was a foot taller than her. "Dad's doing all he can to protect you and make sure no authorities know you're here. It's not your job to worry about him."

Grace and Braxton continued walking down the sidewalk.

"How long do you think it'll take for Jordan to contact Dad?" Braxton asked a few moments later.

"Sometime tonight, but that's just my guess. How long do you think?" Grace responded, looking straight ahead.

"Sounds very optimistic, Grace. I think he'll contact Dad sometime tomorrow afternoon," Braxton said, rubbing his chin in thought.

"How about we bet on it? If I win, you have to do dishes for a week. And if you win, I'll weed the garden for a week."

Braxton thought over the proposition. "Deal," he declared.

"Get ready to lose, Braxton," Grace said.

"I wouldn't be too confident, Grace," Braxton replied.

"We'll see," Grace said mysteriously. "We'll see."

CHAPTER 22

Jolting awake, Jordan didn't know where he was for a moment. Then the memories flooded back into his mind. Last night, he'd stopped at about two in the morning and fallen asleep under a tree.

Now it was six in the morning.

Ugh, my body hurts from lying on the ground too long. I'm not used to sleeping outdoors anymore.

After taking a few moments to stretch, he slowly stood up. Bones aching and brain telling him to fall back asleep, Jordan knew he had to continue moving, no matter how much his body protested.

Let's see how long I can ride before I grow tired.

Jordan climbed back onto the motorcycle.

An hour outside Boise, Idaho, Jordan felt another hunger pain hit him, this one worse than the last. He was going to pass out if he didn't eat something.

That was really dumb of me not to eat something before I left the detention center.

Passing through a small town, Jordan saw a grocery store. He silently celebrated that now he could eat something other than the detention center's awful food.

Checking his back pocket, he was happy to find money. *Thank you, Levi.*

Walking through the store, he wanted to buy everything he saw. After some careful thinking, he grabbed chips, crackers, cookies, grapes, two red apples, an orange, and a couple bottles of water.

As he passed the self-care section, blond hair dye caught his eye. *I miss my original hair color.*

Standing in the checkout line, he noticed a couple people staring at him. He knew he looked like a freak because his hair was long and unkempt; his skin was ghostly white, as if he hadn't seen the sun in a long time; and he hadn't shaved in a while, but he really didn't care. *I'm pretty used to being gawked at all the time. Nothing new.*

At this point, Jordan only cared about two things: eating some food and riding to Boise.

Once back on the motorcycle, Jordan opened the chip bag and ate a few while he sat and people-watched.

I wish my life was as simple as theirs. Their only concern is how to fit into society and not get made fun of.

After a few more minutes of watching, he knew he needed to decide his next step. *I might as well call Levi and tell him where I am. That way he can be prepared to meet me somewhere in Boise.*

It took a few minutes, but he finally found a place that still had a working pay phone. He pulled the piece of paper from his backpack and dialed Levi's number.

"Levi Greenfield speaking," Levi's voice said.

Relief flooded Jordan's mind. "Hey, Levi, it's Jordan. I'm about an hour away from Boise."

"The plan went smoothly, I assume?" Levi questioned. "You didn't get caught by the guards?"

"No, why would I?" Jordan asked, smiling. "I've escaped from the authorities before, and I'll keep doing it until either I'm dead or my mission is complete. I just needed your help this time around. The plan we created was child's play. I've had to deal with plans that were worse than ours."

Levi laughed. "Why does that not surprise me one bit?"

"You know me better than most people do, Levi," reminded Jordan.

"I guess so," responded Levi. "Call me when you're in Boise, and I'll wait for you at the small grassy area on the northeast corner of Main and Sixth."

"All right, I'll see you in about an hour."

One uneventful hour later, Jordan arrived on Boise's Main Street.

I better be much more cautious now. I can't go back to the detention center. I've worked so hard to get this far, and nothing's going to make me go back.

Jordan parked his motorcycle on the side of the road. Instantly, he found Levi, Braxton, and a young woman he didn't recognize sitting on the lawn in front of a car.

Smiling, Jordan walked over.

"How was your ride here?" Braxton asked.

"Not that exciting, if I'm being honest," Jordan said, giving Braxton a huge bear hug.

Braxton laughed.

Jordan turned to the young woman standing next to Levi. "You must be Grace," he said, smiling.

"Yeah, I'm Grace, and you must be Jordan," Grace said warmly, smiling as she walked up to him. "I've been told a lot about you and how we're twins." Tears formed in Grace's eyes.

My twin is standing in front of me. After all these years, I'm able to see her in person. Jordan reached out for Grace and hugged her tightly. *I missed her so much. I wish I could've made this reunion happen sooner.*

He felt her shake in his arms as they continued hugging. "It's all right, Grace. I'm right here," he whispered soothingly.

Grace sniffled, then whispered back, "I know, Jordan. Please don't leave again."

Her words stunned Jordan. *She actually wants me to stay? She cares about me?* Tears pricked the corners of his eyes as he continued hugging Grace. "I will never leave you again, Grace. That's a promise."

Grace hugged him tighter in response.

Once they were both able to contain their emotions, they released their tight embrace, but Jordan kept his arm around Grace.

Levi and Braxton had big smiles on their faces.

"You two are finally reunited, after all these years," Levi said happily.

Jordan and Grace smiled at each other, but didn't respond.

Jordan knew this was where he was meant to be.

■■■■■■■■■■■■■■■■■■

"Braxton, you owe me," Grace said as the four of them sat in the living room of Levi's home.

Braxton groaned. "I know I do."

What are they even talking about? Jordan looked at Grace and Braxton with a perplexed expression.

"Care to explain what's going on here?" Levi asked, raising an eyebrow.

"Grace and I made a bet on how long it would take for Jordan to contact you," Braxton explained bitterly. "Grace bet sometime today, and I bet tomorrow afternoon. So, Grace won."

Jordan laughed, shaking his head in amusement. "Braxton, you were always bad at betting. No wonder Grace won."

Braxton threw a shoe at Jordan, but Jordan caught it.

"Nice reflexes," Grace said, shooting a glare at Braxton.

"What?" Braxton asked. "He caught it, so why are you glaring at me?"

"Jordan's just going to throw it back at you," Grace said slyly. "And he's stronger than you."

Braxton laughed, but also threw up his hands. "Why do you gang up on me?"

"Because it's fun," Grace said sweetly.

Braxton and Grace continued to bicker back and forth. When Grace gave Jordan a slight nod, he knew what she wanted him to do. Trying to suppress a smile and act normal, he threw the shoe at Braxton.

"Ow!" Braxton exclaimed, rubbing his chest.

"Hey, now, let's not get too rowdy," said Levi.

"Here's a lesson for you, Braxton," said Jordan. "Never let yourself get distracted, and never let your guard down."

"I'll make sure to remember that," Braxton muttered. Then he stood up and went upstairs to his room, still rubbing his chest where the shoe had hit him.

"Did you throw it hard or something?" Grace questioned, playfully poking Jordan in his side.

"I didn't throw it *that* hard," Jordan responded, grinning as he wrapped an arm around Grace's shoulder.

For the next hour, the three of them talked about what had been happening in their lives. When Jordan stifled a yawn, Grace stood up and said, "How about I show you to your room?"

"Sounds wonderful. I could use a shower and then sleep for the next eight years."

Grace laughed. "Follow me, then." When they reached the second floor, she pointed and said, "That's Dad's room, the next one is Braxton's, and then there's a guest room. Across the hall is my room, then another guest room, and then your room."

"That's a lot of bedrooms," commented Jordan as he walked toward his room.

"Six bedrooms on the second floor, and two more downstairs that could also be guest rooms," Grace explained.

Jordan was even more impressed when he entered his bedroom. "This is very nice," he said in awe.

"I bet it's a lot nicer than a cell," Grace commented, standing in the doorway.

"Nicer than any room I've been in for a *very* long time," responded Jordan, turning around to face Grace.

"I'll let you get settled in," Grace said before leaving.

Jordan closed his bedroom door. *I better take advantage of this luxury while it lasts.* Slipping off his shirt, he went into his bathroom and turned on the shower. Waiting for steam to rise, he studied himself in the mirror. *I really need to shave my face.*

Climbing into the shower, he let the warm water pelt his skin for a good twenty minutes before grabbing the soap and washing his body. By the time he finished, the water was turning cold. After he shaved and put on clean clothing, he looked in the mirror and felt satisfied.

Feeling hungry, Jordan went downstairs to the kitchen. Levi was sitting at the kitchen table. "There's leftover pizza in the fridge for you," he said, looking up from his phone.

"Awesome!" Jordan exclaimed.

As the pizza was microwaving, Levi said, "I noticed your hair is slowly turning back to blond."

"Yeah, I'm letting it grow out," Jordan said. "It should be fully platinum blond after my next haircut."

"Your natural color is platinum blond?" Braxton asked, walking into the kitchen.

"It was dirty blond at first, but over time it got lighter and lighter," Jordan said, sitting down at the kitchen table with his plate of pizza. "It got to where it looked white when I was outside."

"That's crazy," Braxton said.

Jordan nodded, his mouth full of pizza.

"What's crazy?" Grace asked, entering the kitchen.

"Jordan used to have dirty blond hair, and then it became platinum blond over time," Braxton explained.

"Oh yeah," Grace said, "I vaguely remember you having really blond hair that turned white in the sun."

"You do?" Jordan asked, almost choking on his pizza.

"Yeah, I remember that," Grace answered. She sat down next
to Jordan and ripped a piece of crust from his pizza.

Levi, Jordan, Braxton, and Grace talked late into the night.

"You three better head off to bed," Levi finally said, getting up from the kitchen table. "Braxton and Grace, Henry's father will pick you up for school, since I don't get off work till late afternoon."

"All right, Dad," Braxton and Grace said in unison.

In his room, Jordan opened a window, turned off the lights, and lay back onto his bed. Looking up at the ceiling, he heard an occasional car drive past.

Today's been a good day—very long, but good.
He soon fell asleep. For the first time in a long time, he didn't have any nightmares.

CHAPTER 23

Jordan woke up early the next morning, though he was still very tired. His phone said seven-fifteen. *I might as well get up. There's no point going back to sleep.*

Climbing out of bed, he pulled on his jeans and shirt from the night before.

Breakfast was ready by the time Jordan got downstairs, and he noticed that Grace was in the living room with another boy.

Who is that?

Both Grace and the mysterious boy looked up when he entered the room.

The boy looked shocked. "I don't mean to be rude or anything, but what happened to your arms and neck?"

"You didn't say anything rude. I was burned." Jordan grinned slightly.

The boy laughed and shook Jordan's hand. "I'm Henry," he said.

"Nice to meet you, Henry. I'm Jordan."

Henry's eyes widened. "You mean you're *the* Jordan? The Jordan in the news?"

"Yeah, I guess," Jordan said.

"Well, my dad's waiting in the car," Henry said, getting up from the couch.

"All right, let me grab my backpack," Grace said, walking into the kitchen. "Braxton, time to go."

"It was really nice to meet you, Jordan," Henry said over his shoulder as he headed to the front door.

"It was nice to meet you, too, Henry," Jordan said.

Braxton and Grace came out of the kitchen a few moments later.

"I'll see you two later then?" Jordan asked, raising an eyebrow.

"No doubt about that," Braxton said happily.

Smiling, Jordan lightly punched Braxton on the arm. Turning to Grace, he hugged her and whispered in her ear, "Be safe. I'll pick you and Braxton up after school. Just text or call me."

Hugging Jordan, Grace whispered back, "I'm usually safe, Jordan. But I'll try to be safe, anyways. I'll let you know when we get out of school."

"Thank you, Grace."

Grace didn't respond, just gave him a slight smile before walking out the door.

I hope Levi won't mind if I pick up Grace and Braxton from school.

Jordan stared at the front door, alone in the huge house.

In the kitchen, Jordan looked for something to eat. Blasting music on full volume, he danced around as he moved from fridge to cupboard and pantry.

Suddenly, Jordan lost his hunger for no apparent reason. He stopped dancing. His body shook, and his breath became shallow and labored.

Not this again.

He tried to breathe normally. Resisting the urge to throw up, Jordan sat down on the kitchen floor, head between his knees.

Not another panic attack. Not another one. I don't need to deal with this right now.

Almost in an instant, Levi was at Jordan's side, eyes full of concern. "Jordan, what's wrong?" he asked.

Jordan shook his head, not able to respond.

"Panic attack?" Levi questioned.

Jordan nodded.

Levi bit his lip, but didn't say anything as he continued watching Jordan shake.

I wish the panic attacks would just go away forever.

Once Jordan's body stopped shaking and he didn't feel like he was going to throw up, he told Levi what had happened.

"I was just going about my day, finding something for breakfast and listening to my music, when all of a sudden I lost my appetite, felt like I was going to throw up, and started shaking. That's when you came home."

Taking Jordan's hand, Levi helped him stand up. "I'm not surprised you're having panic attacks with all you've been through recently. Why don't you sit down and I'll make you some breakfast."

"I'm not hungry, though," Jordan protested.

"You need to have something," Levi said in a warning tone. "You've hardly eaten since you got here."

"All right, I'll try," Jordan said dejectedly, pulling out a chair at the kitchen table.

Levi prepared a bowl of cereal and set it in front of Jordan, giving him a look that said *Eat the cereal.*

Jordan knew he wouldn't get very far arguing with Levi, so he picked up the spoon with a slightly shaking hand and began to slowly eat.

Levi stood in the kitchen, watching to make sure Jordan ate.

I don't know why Levi's being so concerned about me. I'm perfectly fine now.

"You're awfully quiet," Levi said.

"I'm thinking, that's all," Jordan said, setting down the spoon.

"About what?" asked Levi, leaning against the counter.

"How you don't need to be concerned for me," Jordan said. "I've been taking care of myself for years."

"Sometimes it's good to let others take care of you, even if you're more than capable of taking care of yourself," said Levi.

"I know," said Jordan. "It's just . . . I don't want to make your life harder than it already is."

"Jordan, you're not making my life harder. I genuinely care about you and your well-being. If you're not happy, then I'm not happy, and that goes for Braxton and Grace, too. I knew the risks of taking on three teenagers at once, but I know that's what I'm supposed to do. Even if two of the teenagers are prisoners who escaped with my help," Levi added with a smile.

"How am I not making your life harder? I put your job at risk!" Jordan felt anger rising inside him.

"Jordan," Levi said calmly. "The only reason I was working there was to keep an eye on you and help you break out."

"What do you mean?" Jordan asked.

Levi sighed. "Both Elijah and I were assigned to keep an eye on you at different times. Elijah couldn't do it very long because he was a guard and had to keep up that appearance, and plus you ran away. Once we found out where you were, I was assigned to watch you. Lots of others have been keeping an eye on you, too, from a distance."

"Why all this surveillance?" Jordan questioned.

"Because you, Jordan, are a very important person to keep alive," Levi said seriously. "You're the only one who's survived Adrian's experiments and can handle all those powers."

"I have powers?" Jordan asked, confused.

"You didn't know that?" Levi asked, eyes flashing with concern.

"No, I don't know about any powers," Jordan said.

Tilting his head, Levi asked, "Have you ever noticed that your strength regenerates faster than the average person? And you can run extremely fast and for a long time? And your brain works a *lot* faster? And your hearing is so sensitive that you can hear almost everything?"

"I've noticed when I'm running from police or gangs, they can't keep up with me. They end up losing me, but I just thought they were out of shape. And I never realized my brain works a lot faster than an ordinary human. I do remember when I've had to think up a plan or a way to escape under pressure, but what does that have to do with . . ." Jordan fell silent as the truth hit him. *That's why Adrian wants me so badly. Because I have powers. I'm a superhuman. A mutant.*

"You might have even more powers, Jordan. When the right time comes, additional powers might unlock." Levi rubbed his chin.

"Is there a way to find out, like tests or something?" Jordan asked.

Levi paused before answering. "It's possible. I'd have to talk to my boss and see if the scientists could work with you."

"It'd be interesting to see what I'm capable of," Jordan said calmly.

"I'll speak with my boss tonight. Hopefully, we can help you find answers. For now, don't tell Grace or Braxton. Just keep it between you and me."

"Of course, Levi. The fewer who know about my special abilities, the better."

"Excellent," Levi said, stifling a yawn. "I'm going to go shower and take a nap. I'll talk to you again before I leave."

Jordan remained at the kitchen table, thinking.

CHAPTER 24

"So, Jordan had no idea about his powers?" Josiah asked on the phone after Levi explained what he'd learned about Jordan.

"Adrian never mentioned anything at all about powers to Jordan," Levi said, tapping a pen on the desk. "Nobody ever did."

"Are there signs that he could possibly have more powers?" Josiah questioned.

"When he gets angry, sometimes I see what appear to be sparks of some sort in his eyes," Levi recalled. "I don't know what that means entirely, but it could be a sign of some sort of electrical power. Other times, I see flames burning inside his eyes."

"Jordan could have more powers than what we're all seeing," said Josiah. "Is he willing to come in tomorrow night so my scientists can look at him?"

"That should work. He's gotten curious about his powers. I

promised him I'd talk to you and see what your thoughts are."

"Bring him in tomorrow," Josiah said before ending the call.

I hope all goes well.

Levi nervously drove Jordan to the science facility. "You all right, Jordan? You've been awfully quiet all day."

"I'm fine," Jordan said simply.

"You sure?" Levi questioned, looking at Jordan again.

"Yes, I'm sure, Levi. Just nervous."

Levi almost asked the boy why he would be nervous, but then he thought he knew why. *Dr. Adrian's scientists must have done some pretty awful experiments on him if he's now afraid of all scientists and doctors.*

"These scientists aren't like the ones Dr. Adrian has," Levi assured Jordan. "They don't conduct experiments that kill or hurt people. They'll be gentle with you."

"That's what Dr. Adrian told me," Jordan responded angrily, sparks flashing in his eyes. "I believed him, and look where that got me."

Sparks in his eyes probably aren't a good sign.

"Jordan," Levi said kindly, "do you think I'd ever hurt you?"

Jordan was silent for a moment. "No, I don't think you'd ever hurt me."

Levi sighed with relief. *I'm glad at least I have his trust.*

"But saying they'll be gentle—words like that haunt my memory," Jordan murmured. "They were spoken by a man I trusted with my life. A man who took responsibility to help me and then broke me."

"Jordan—I'm so sorry. I didn't know. If I did, I would've worded it differently."

"Dad, it's not your fault. You didn't know because I didn't tell you," Jordan whispered.

"What else have they done to you?" Levi questioned, instantly dreading the response he might get.

To his surprise, all Jordan said was, "I don't want to talk about it. The less you know, the better."

▬▬▬▬▬▬▬▬▬▬▬▬▬▬▬▬▬

"Jordan, are you ready? Levi called from the bottom of the stairs.

"Oh, did Jordan not tell you?" Braxton asked, coming down the stairs.

"Tell me what?"

"He went to school early today."

That would make sense. He's been pretty nervous about school. Probably wasn't a good time to bring it up after he met with the scientists last night.

"Well, let's go then," Levi said, loud enough for Grace to hear in the kitchen. "Don't want to be late."

▬▬▬▬▬▬▬▬▬▬▬▬▬▬▬▬▬

Jordan was nervous the entire day. He didn't have Grace or Braxton in any classes, and he wasn't keen on trying to make friends at the moment.

I hope I can find Grace or Braxton during lunch.

When the lunch bell finally rang, Jordan walked out of his psychology class. To his surprise, Braxton passed by just then.

"I haven't seen you at all today," Braxton said as Jordan joined him. "I was getting used to hanging around you all the time."

"Hmm, I wonder why," Jordan responded, rolling his eyes.

"Yeah, I wonder why," Braxton retorted.

The two boys continued down the hallway. Jordan felt his dog-tag necklace clank against his denim-jacket buttons as he walked.

"Just to warn you," said Braxton, "we're sitting with some of Grace's friends."

"Okay, thanks for the warning."

Nearing the table, Jordan saw three boys sitting around Grace. His immediate reaction was that they were harassing her, but then he realized they were the friends Braxton had mentioned.

After Grace introduced Jordan, the pale boy—James—asked, "Aren't you that escaped prisoner from the news?"

"You better not turn me in, or I'll hunt you down," Jordan said, trying to act mean.

It seemed to work, because the pale boy stuttered, "I won't t-t-turn you in—j-j-just please don't hurt me."

Smiling, Jordan walked over to Grace, pulled her up, and gave her a big bear hug. The boys looked at Jordan and Grace like they were crazy.

"Jordan's my twin," Grace mumbled, while being crushed by Jordan's arms.

"Oh, that makes sense," Theodore said. "I wondered why he was hugging you."

"Nice to see you again, Henry," Jordan said, nodding at Henry.

"Same," Henry said, smiling at Jordan.

"You two've already met?" James asked.

"Just the other day," Jordan said, sitting down on Grace's left.

"How come you didn't tell us?" Theo asked, looking at Henry with a hurt expression.

"Because you two would've freaked out," Henry responded simply, not looking up from his sandwich.

"You know us so well," James muttered under his breath.

Though James was sitting across the table in the noisy cafeteria, Jordan heard his mumbled words perfectly, which reminded him of yesterday. *Don't think about it too much. You'll just start worrying again.*

"So, Jordan, how long have you been in Boise?" Henry asked.

"Almost a week."

The three boys looked surprised. "Why haven't we seen you around, then?" James asked, his brows furrowed.

"I had to lay low for a few days," Jordan said. "You know—the police."

"Let's go get some food," Braxton said to Jordan.

The rest of the day went by slowly. After school, Jordan met Braxton, Grace, and her three friends. They chatted for a while, but then Jordan needed to be alone for a minute. "I gotta hit the john," he said.

To Jordan's dismay, Henry followed him into the restroom. *I just hope he doesn't ask me questions.*

As they both washed their hands, Henry asked, "So, when you were at the detention center, what did they do to you if you didn't cooperate?"

"Well, I never cooperated, so they sedated me whenever an officer came into my cell, because I'd hospitalized a few. I think I even killed a couple."

Henry looked at Jordan like he was crazy.

That's just one of many looks I get when I answer questions honestly.

"Hey, can I see your burns and scars?" Henry asked. "I've heard a lot about them."

Jordan smiled. "Are you sure? They're pretty gnarly."

Henry nodded and braced himself.

Sighing, Jordan removed his jacket. After a deep breath to calm his nerves, he slowly pulled off his long-sleeved T-shirt. *I hope it doesn't gross him out too much.*

Henry looked like he was going to pass out.

Jordan's burns and cuts were most severe on his back, where Dr. Adrian had found the easiest access for punishing him.

"I told you it was bad," Jordan said.

"Define bad," Henry said, shaking his head.

Jordan turned to face Henry. "I got these before I went to the detention center."

"Does Levi know about these?" Henry asked.

"Yes and no. He knows about the ones on my arms, but not the rest of my body. I wasn't planning on telling him."

"I think you should tell," Henry said, folding his arms, "so he's aware of all that's happened to you."

Jordan didn't say anything as he put his shirt and jacket back on. *I hope he doesn't tell Levi.*

Exiting the restroom, Jordan noticed several girls by the drinking fountain.

They all looked at him and seemed to be trying not to laugh.

"Hi, Jordan, I'm Ivy," one of them said, stepping towards him. "You're the new hot topic of the school."

"Oh, yeah?" Jordan said.

The girls laughed like he'd told a joke.

"You should hang out with us," Ivy said. "You're popular-kid material, unlike Henry here, who betrayed his own kind." She
frowned at Henry.

Jordan thought about it. "Thanks, but I think I'll stick with the group I'm with now."

The girl's face instantly looked like she'd sucked on a lemon.

Jordan motioned to Henry, and the two of them walked away, not looking back. *Hopefully I won't have to deal with those girls again.*

After they turned a corner, Jordan glanced over at Henry. "Why are you smiling?" he asked, breaking the silence between them.

"Well, you're one of the few people who didn't fall into the popular kid trap," said Henry. "I did at one point, but I got back onto the right track, thanks to your sister."

"It was really easy," said Jordan. "I knew what they were trying to do. And it's apparently easy for me to make people angry and make them hate me."

"Why do you think that, Jordan?" asked Henry. "Levi never seemed ticked off when he was trying to work with you. He told me you're very stubborn. That's why nobody wanted to work with you."

"More than half the authorities thought I was a lost cause," muttered Jordan quietly. "I've been broken down since I was ten, and I'm still broken and can never be fixed. Everyone who's met me or knows me hates me in some way. That's why I have very few friends and very few people I can trust."

Henry fell silent.

This was all Jordan needed. He just needed to tell someone what was on his mind and for that person to just listen and not try to offer advice.

"Henry, did I ever tell you how good of a friend you are to Grace, Braxton, and me?" Jordan asked, filling the silence.

Henry smiled. "Not until now. I'm glad."

The two boys made their way outside to the gathering tree. When they arrived, Grace was talking.

"What are you guys talking about?" Henry asked as he and Jordan sat down on the grass.

"I was just starting to tell them about Jordan's backstory," Grace said. Glancing at Jordan, she added, "I hope you don't mind."

Jordan shrugged. "Go ahead, I don't mind. I want to see what you get right."

"All right, if you say so," Grace said hesitantly. "According to Jordan's file, he ran away from home when he was eight, survived on his own for two years before Dr. Adrian took him in, left Dr. Adrian and got into a bad group of teens, stole stuff, and got put in the youth detention center. Four years later, Dr. Adrian bailed him out and took him back in. He worked with Dr. Adrian for years, got tortured, ran away again, got put back into detention, and broke out."

Jordan raised an eyebrow in surprise. "How did you remember all that?"

"I don't know, I just did," Grace responded, playing with a string on her jacket.

"Most of that's right, but let me fill in the rest, just for kicks and giggles," Jordan said, smirking. "Let's start with my childhood. Like most people, we had loving parents who would take us to the park, play games with us, and take us out to eat. When we were eight, our parents were murdered and I ran away. I regret leaving Grace behind, but I was traumatized and wanted to get as far away as I could. I survived on my own for four years and made a few friends and helped them survive for a while, but then the officers found our hiding place and we had to run. My friends and I got separated. I'm pretty sure most of them ended up in jail."

Changing position, Jordan stretched out his legs. The others sat still with wide eyes, waiting for more. "Dr. Adrian found me almost dead on the side of the road," Jordan continued. "He was like a dad to me. He cared for me while I was recovering and afterwards, too. Dr. Adrian taught me combat, survival, and how to use a gun, flamethrower, knife, and some more complicated and dangerous weapons. Then I had to prove I was loyal and committed to kill when necessary. I'd killed animals, but when Dr. Adrian ordered me to kill an actual human being, I told him he was crazy. I busted out of the building and hid for a while. Dr. Adrian found me a couple months later, and that's when he tortured me for the first time. I broke out again and ran for my life. I then stole from a store and ended up back in detention until I met Levi. And you all know the rest of the story."

I'm not going to give them the rest of the details. They don't need to know.

Later, Braxton was telling a different story when Jordan felt sudden pain. He grabbed his head and groaned. The others asked Jordan what was wrong, but their voices were muddled.

He started to shake and felt his sweat pour down his body. After a few moments, he passed out.

When he came to, everything was buzzing all around him. He could hear birds chirping and kids playing near the end of the road in a driveway.

Sitting up, Jordan looked around.

He was in the neighborhood where he'd almost died. He knew he had to get out of there fast. Something bad was going to happen, just like the first time he'd experienced it.

Jordan jumped up when he saw the gang of boys. He knew they couldn't see him, but it felt so real. When he saw a younger version of himself standing nearby, he knew he was only there to watch. He couldn't change the past.

"You're on our turf," one of the gang members said.

Young Jordan said, "I don't see a sign anywhere, dummy."

The gang member got up into Jordan's face.

Jordan said defiantly, "You can never take me down, you big, dumb monkey." Then he punched the gang member, making his nose bleed.

The other gang members attacked Jordan. One punch hit him in the eye. There was a flash of light, and then Jordan couldn't see out of that eye.

"What do you think about that?" the gang leader asked, drawing out a knife and holding it to Jordan's neck.

"Do you really want my opinion? Or are you talking to your gang of baboons?"

"That's it! I'll teach you a lesson you'll never forget!" The gang leader's face was red.

"That's what another gang leader said," Jordan said, attempting to shrug his shoulders, despite being pinned by another boy. "It didn't work."

The gang leader paused. "Which gang leader?"

"I don't remember," Jordan said.

"What did he look like?" the gang leader asked.

"He was short and fat and had a spike on his belt buckle." As Jordan continued listing details, the gang leader's face grew paler.

"You're very lucky you survived him, then," the gang leader said quietly.

Jordan raised an eyebrow. "Why do you say that?"

"Because he killed off most of my gang, including my brother," the gang leader murmured.

Jordan's body went numb as he remembered a kid who'd looked a lot like this gang leader. "I knew your brother really well," Jordan said shakily. "I saw him get killed right in front of me."

The gang leader looked surprised. "You did?"

Jordan nodded. Just then, a stab of pain shot down his spine and he winced.

"Wait—I recognize you!" the gang leader said excitedly. "You're Jordan!"

"Yeah, that's me," Jordan said.

"Dang, you look so different since I saw you last. It's been—what, two years now?" the gang leader asked.

"More than two years," Jordan responded.

The gang leader thought for a moment. "Yeah, it has." Looking at his baboons, the leader said, "Guys, let him go."

They reluctantly released Jordan and walked back to their leader's side.

"I tried to save your brother," Jordan explained. "I saved him from the cops, saved him from practically everything—except for that night when the murderer came. I almost died that night, but your brother saved me. I tried to get the murderer to follow me, but he was set on killing your brother. I've never forgiven myself. I should've been a better friend to him."

The gang leader didn't say anything for a while. Finally, he said, "I'll let you go. But just know that this is the only time. You better step off my turf before I change my mind."

Jordan watched his younger self walk away. His heart ached, remembering the night one of his best friends was murdered. As he stood there, he felt himself leaving the memory and moving back into the real world.

CHAPTER 25

When Jordan finally woke up, he was lying in a hospital bed. He noticed an IV sticking out of his arm and he could feel a bandage around his head.

A few minutes later, a nurse came into the room, followed by Levi.

Great, I'm going to get a lecture.

"Jordan, your dad's here to see you," the nurse said, stating the obvious.

Sitting up, Jordan nodded. The nurse left the room, leaving Jordan and Levi alone.

"Jordan, what happened? I got a frantic call from Grace that you passed out, so I called an ambulance."

"How long have I been here?" Jordan asked, ignoring Levi's question.

"A day. Jordan, what happened?"

"I've been stuck in here a whole day?!"

"Yes. Now answer my question. What happened?" Levi repeated, this time stubbornly.

"Dad, I can't explain it—I just can't," Jordan said, lying back down.

"Well, give it your best try and I'll try to make sense of what you're saying," Levi said, a hint of pleading in his voice.

Jordan shook his head and looked away from Levi. *What I'm going through is only for me to know.*

"Jordan, I want to help you, but I need to know what happened," Levi said, sitting down on the bed.

"I have flashbacks from my past," Jordan said. "Things I should've done better in my life. It's horrible, but I have to go through it. I have to live and face my consequences."

"Grace said you were muttering, something like, 'I was friends with your brother and I tried to save him.' And you have some gashes on the back of your head, most likely from when you fell."

"Dad, I'm sorry I didn't tell you sooner about the flashbacks," Jordan said, looking away from Levi. "I didn't think they'd be this big a problem."

A doctor came in with a clipboard. Something about him seemed familiar to Jordan, but he couldn't place him.

"I'll be back here tonight," Levi said, standing up to leave. "Braxton's coming with me."

"So, Jordan, how are you feeling today?" asked the doctor.

"I feel a little lightheaded and dizzy, and my head hurts." Jordan winced as he touched the bandage.

The doctor made a note and then walked over to a medical cabinet, returning with a syringe full of clear liquid. "This'll help your lightheadedness and dizziness. And it'll take the edge off so I can inspect your headwound. I tried this yesterday, and you punched me."

"Sorry, I must have been delirious," Jordan said apologetically.

"No problem—this time I'm prepared," the doctor said, laughing.

Smiling, Jordan let the doctor do his thing. He felt a little prick above his collarbone. The doctor then unwrapped Jordan's bandages and waited for the medicine to kick in.

When Jordan woke up, he found a new doctor sitting in the chair next to his bed. The doctor's face was very familiar. *Where have I met this guy before?*

Then Jordan remembered who it was. "Hey, Jace, how are you doing?" he asked, starting to sit up.

"I'm doing well. Did you make it out of the detention center okay, again?" Jace questioned.

"Yeah, thanks to some help from my foster dad. Did you get out okay, that time I was in detention with you?" Jordan asked.

"Yeah, along with Wyatt. We're now undercover doctors here assigned by Josiah Hale, who works with the Academy. Wyatt was your doctor from last night and also the day before, when you punched him. He was the one who injected the flashback serum into you before he looked at your headwound."

Jordan nodded but felt confused. "That was flashback serum? I don't remember very much from my past, other than a few scenes and snippets from way long ago."

Now Jace looked confused. "Do you remember anything

from our Academy days together, when we were learning to be spies?"

"I remember you guys. But that was six years ago, before I was sent on my mission to get inside Dr. Adrian's craziness. I only recall random snippets from that time," Jordan said, straining his memory.

"I can help you with that," said Jace. "I'll just need to be in a memory with you, so I can explain what's going on. Then you'll understand what's happening to your life. But you can't remember anything?"

"Hardly anything," Jordan said, shaking his head. "It's like my memories have been sucked out of me."

"Hmm. I can still show you all you need to know about your past. And I think I'm going to right now."

Jace stepped out and then returned with Wyatt. Following Jace's instructions, the three of them strapped each other into metal chairs and injected serum into each other's arms. Then they waited for what came next.

At first, Jordan saw pitch black all around him. Then he saw the three of them on a train with other young people. "So, Jordan, at the time of this memory, none of us have met yet," said Jace. "Earlier, you got into a fight with one of our friends, so everyone is staying away from you. The train is about to pull up to the Academy's train station, until suddenly the train stops."

Jordan glanced at Jace. "You don't need to tell me everything we see. I can see it for myself. I'll ask you when I need you to clarify something."

Jace nodded, remaining quiet.

Jordan watched his younger self look out the window. Another train was already in the station with crowds of people getting off. Before long, their train was able to pull into the station. When Jordan disembarked, he noticed an elderly man waiting nearby.

"You must be Jordan Thurgood," said the elderly man with a slight British accent.

"Yes, I am, sir, and your name is?" the young Jordan questioned.

"I'm the man who brought you here to the Academy of Spies. My name isn't important at the moment. This might sound strange, but I need you to lead an army. I know you have the potential to do it."

"You brought me here?" replied young Jordan. "I'm surprised you'd be interested in someone living on the streets."

"Yes, I did. Some of my former students have been watching you and recommended you to me. They told me a bit about you and your personality. From the sound of it, you'll be a good leader with the right training. If you succeed, you'll stay in this school. And if you don't—well, you'll go back to your family and live your normal life. Am I clear?"

"Yes, sir. I'll try my hardest in all my training," young Jordan said.

"Good, I knew I could count on you. Now, go to your dorm and sleep well. Tomorrow will be very busy for you."

Young Jordan nodded and followed an escort down a long hallway to a dormitory.

In the room, there were ten boys, each assigned a cot where they'd sleep for the rest of their training days. Jordan found his nametag on a cot between two boys who he could tell were friends from the way they talked and joked with each other.

"So, you made it this far, huh?" said the boy whose nametag said Wyatt. "We saw the headmaster talking to you on the platform, and he didn't look happy. We thought he was going to send you back home for fighting with our friend."

"Yeah, he just talked to me, that's all," young Jordan said.

"About what?" questioned another boy, named Jace.

"It's none of your concern. It's just between the headmaster and me."

"Well, you're no fun. If we have to share a dorm with you, we might as well get to know you," Wyatt said.

"I'm pretty sure you have. I'm the one who messed up your friend over there." Jordan gestured across the room towards a boy with a black eye.

"Right, anyway, my name is Jace, and this is Wyatt," Jace said, pointing at Wyatt.

Why don't they just get the hint that I don't want to be friends and stop talking to me?

Jordan nodded, not saying anything, and fell onto his cot. As the other boys talked, he kept to himself. He hoped that he seemed cold, hard, mean, and distant to the other boys.

"You might as well get to know us," said Jace, sitting down on his cot next to Jordan. "I heard from kids who've been training here a couple years that you need to have some friends. The headmaster finds people you aren't friends with and makes you fight them. The more friends you have, the harder it is for him to find someone. But I heard he's changing it this year."

"That'll be the last thing I do," Jordan replied, looking up. "I don't need to get to know anybody. We're just going to have to fight our friends, anyway."

Jace nodded. Wyatt came over and said, "You know, word's spreading that you're the best fighter the school's ever seen. Apparently someone saw a note in your file that you're a really good fighter. You could give us some pointers. Our fighting, agility, and knowledge scores determine if we stay in the school or get kicked out."

Nodding, Jordan said, "It might be nice to have a couple guys to teach."

"We already know we suck at fighting," Wyatt said. "We don't want to get kicked out. I know my parents would be disappointed if I didn't stay here long enough to learn something. They spent a lot of time helping me get in. And I really want to stay here."

"All right, I'll train you," said Jordan. "Just don't tell anyone."

The two guys nodded and followed Jordan out to the training grounds.

A few weeks later, everyone in the whole school was talking about how good both Jace and Wyatt had gotten at fighting.

By that time, Jordan had a crush on one of the girls in his classes. One day Jace asked him, "You seem distracted this morning. Is your mind still on Emma?"

"Yeah, I can't get her out of my mind," Jordan said, shaking his head. "It's been driving me crazy."

"Just go talk to her," Jace said, sitting down on the grass next to Jordan. "You'll never get to know her unless you talk to her."

"You know Jace is right," Wyatt said, sitting on Jordan's other side.

"I know, but I'm just thinking about what to say to her," Jordan said.

Jace and Wyatt shook their heads. Getting up from the grass, Jordan started walking towards an outside area with tables and chairs.

"Where are you going?" Jace asked. "We still have an hour before dinner."

"I know. I'm just going to talk to someone," Jordan said over his shoulder.

Jordan walked down a pathway towards where Emma usually hung out. He saw her sitting in a chair underneath a tree and went over to her.

It's either now or never. I better do it, or I'm going to regret it later.

"Hey, Emma, can I sit here?" asked Jordan, gesturing to the chair across from her.

Emma smiled. "Sure, it's yours, if you want it. I just came here to get away from my friends."

Jordan smiled and sat right across from Emma. Instead of saying something witty, he said, "Emma, I like you."

Emma looked at Jordan for a moment, and Jordan's face went bright red. He wanted to smack himself. *Why would I say that to her?! Well, now it's too late.* He shifted in his chair.

"Jordan, I like you, too, and I really mean it. I was going to say that to you, but you said it first. Not a lot of guys make the first move. I've had a lot of guys say they like me, but I feel a connection with you. I think we could be friends."

Jordan grabbed her hand, and they looked at each other for a moment.

Jordan suddenly found himself in reality again. "What happened after that?" he asked.

"Well, you and Emma started a friendship and then a relationship," said Jace. "But then they gave you a spy mission."

Jordan nodded. "I remember something else. The headmaster said I'd be taking a bigger risk than any spy in history. He had a
plan for me, and I agreed to it. That's what happened to my life!"

After thinking for a few moments, Jordan explained to Jace and Wyatt, "The headmaster told me I'd lose my memory so I wouldn't reveal myself to our enemies. The anti-memory serum was injected into me, making me forget everything from my past. I need to talk to the headmaster!"

"That's why you were being weird about your memories," Wyatt said, nodding. "This actually makes sense."

"Right now, we can't find the headmaster," said Jace. "When we lost all location on you, the headmaster told us to go find you. Emma insisted that she come with us, but the headmaster said she had a different role to play in this plan. A few months ago, we tried to contact the headmaster, but nobody would answer our calls. Either they went into hiding or the school got destroyed."

Emma still wanted to see me? Even after I left? I would think she would've moved on and fallen in love with someone else.

"For now, keep trying the headmaster until your call gets through," said Jordan. "If it doesn't, we'll go to the school and see for ourselves what's going on."

The boys were quiet for a moment, thinking. Finally, Wyatt said, "That's a better idea than what I came up with."

"What was your idea?" Jordan asked.

"That we should just wait for the headmaster or the school to contact us, but that could take months or even years. By then, Dr. Adrian probably would've already taken over the world."

"Let's make that our plan B," said Jordan. "Jace, do you have any ideas?"

"No, not really. For now, let's just go with these two plans."

"Sounds good," Jordan said, grinning at his two best friends.

"The three friends fight against evil again," Wyatt said in a dramatic voice. All of them laughed.

▪▪▪▪▪▪▪▪▪▪▪▪▪▪▪▪▪▪

The next night, Levi and Braxton stopped by Jordan's hospital room.

"Hey, Jordan, how are you feeling?" Braxton said, sitting down in the chair next to the bed.

"I've been through worse," Jordan said, grinning. "The doctors say I can go home in a couple days. They still have to do a few tests and physical exams—you know, the usual protocol."

Braxton asked, "Do you remember Alexis and the other popular kids?"

"How could I forget them?" Jordan said sarcastically.

Braxton laughed. "Today at school, Alexis was freaking out because you weren't there. She blamed Grace for whatever happened to you and started yelling at her. So then, me and the guys had to intervene before things got worse."

"Sounds like I need to get back to school soon," Jordan said.

Braxton nodded. "You know, lunch was pretty lonely without you today. Hopefully you'll get better soon."

"I'll try my best," Jordan said, smiling weakly. The medicine was starting to wear off, and his body was aching again.

"We better let Jordan rest," Levi said to Braxton. Turning to

Jordan, he said, "I'll be back tomorrow morning before you start the routine tests."

"Okay, Dad," Jordan said weakly.

After Levi and Braxton left, Jordan tried to sleep, but he kept tossing and turning as thoughts pummeled his head.

I need something to do, something to get me off my thoughts so hopefully I can sleep.

Jordan stared at the curtains, which were faintly moving because of the vent.

In the middle of the night, a nurse walked in, but it wasn't Jordan's usual nurse. He quickly realized the person wasn't a nurse at all. It was a man with red eyes who wore all black and had jet-black hair.

Jordan stared at the man. His instincts told him to run or fight, but all he could do was lie in the bed and watch helplessly.

"Your name is Jordan, correct?" the man asked, coming closer.

Jordan gave a slight nod and the evil man smiled darkly. "Do you know who sent me?" he asked, sitting down in the chair.

Jordan noticed that the man was wearing a knife pouch and he had on a gun holster under his shirt.

"No, I don't," Jordan said.

"Dr. Adrian sent me to hunt you down." The name filled Jordan with dread. "Not to hurt you—just to bring you back to him."

Jordan knew this was a lie. All Dr. Adrian had ever done to Jordan was hurt him. He would want to do more experiments, and some of the experiments would hurt like torture.

"Do you really think I'd follow you willingly?" Jordan questioned as he stood up from the hospital bed.

"Hmm, I didn't think of it like that. Once you realized who sent me, I thought you'd come willingly."

"Clearly, Dr. Adrian didn't tell you much about me," Jordan said, reaching for something in the blankets.

"Well, then, why don't you tell me a few things about you?" the man asked, sitting up straighter.

"For starters, I don't gladly or willingly follow unknown men without fighting back. Second, you should've searched the room before you sat down." A dark smile crossed Jordan's face.

"What do you mean by that?" the man asked, panic rising in his voice.

"Because I, too, have a weapon."

Jordan threw a knife at the man, hitting him on the right arm. With Jordan's extra strength, the knife cut through the bone and stuck in the wall behind the man him, coated with blood from tip to hilt.

Screaming in anguish, the man held his arm to stop the blood from pouring onto the floor, but it proved useless.

"I noticed that was your dominant arm," Jordan said, retrieving another throwing knife from under his bedding.

"How did you know I'm right-handed?" the man questioned between breaths.

"You closed the door with your right hand, and you holster your gun on the left and carry your knife on the right."

"Dr. Adrian trained you well," the man said in a pained voice. "Maybe even better than himself."

"Oh, I didn't learn that from Dr. Adrian. It was something I taught myself. I've become quite good at noticing small and simple details, along with some complex details as well."

Holding his knife at the man's throat, Jordan took the man's weapons. He then sat and watched the man as he writhed in pain on the floor. Over the next few hours, his noises and movements lessened until he finally died from loss of blood.

It's a shame I had to kill him. If only he'd chosen the right side in this war, he would've lived a longer, better life.

When Jace and Wyatt arrived soon after dawn, Jordan was perched on top of the bed, looking down at the lifeless body without any emotion.

The boys looked at him quizzically. "Did you always have a dead body lying around in here, or is this new?" Jace asked, pointing at the body as he sat down on the chair by Jordan's bed.

"Oh, this is new," Jordan said, unconcerned. "This guy came into my room and said Dr. Adrian ordered him to bring me back. Luckily, I always keep my throwing knifes with me."

"Oh, that seems like a likely reason to have a body in your room," Wyatt said sarcastically.

Jordan rolled his eyes at Wyatt before looking at Jace and asking, "Do you know where we can hide the body?"

"Yeah, we'll just make up a patient record for him and claim he died in his sleep from a chronic health issue," Jace said.

"Sounds like you have it all figured out."

"We came to talk to you before you start the routine tests," Wyatt said, changing the subject. "We advise you to not eat or drink anything too heavy before then. Levi will be here soon so you can spend some time with him. If all the tests come back clear, you could go home tomorrow or the next day. We don't think the tests will show anything serious because your healing powers have probably speeded up the healing process. We'll give you more instructions later."

"Lovely," was all Jordan wanted to say.

■■■■■■■■■■■■■■■■■■

An hour before the first test, Levi came into the room. "You nervous?" he asked as he sat on the bed.

"No, not at all," Jordan said, trying to hide his anxiety. He could tell Levi wasn't buying his act.

"You've gone through a lot of things that would scare others, but don't scare you. You've made it through life-or-death situations, so this will be nothing. Just think of the physical tests as an . . . experiment."

"That's not at all comforting and slightly concerning that you'd call the tests an experiment, considering how much PTSD I have," Jordan said, raising an eyebrow.

Smiling, Levi continued giving Jordan words of encouragement.

■■■■■■■■■■■■■■■■■■

Jordan couldn't recall much about the physical tests, other than that they were long and boring, but now he had throbbing pain from all the different pokes and prods.

Not the worst trial I've had.

When he opened his eyes, Grace and Braxton were sitting at his side.

"How are you feeling?" Grace asked.

"Other than my body hurting, I'm fine," Jordan said. "So, have you both been here the entire time I was asleep?"

"Yes, we have," Grace said, tears welling up in her eyes.

They're very supportive of me. I wish more people in my life were like that.

"Come here," Jordan said, pulling his sister and older brother into a hug. "I want you both with me through any other trial I go through," he declared once Braxton and Grace pulled away.

Smiling, Grace and Braxton gave Jordan another hug.

"I think I'm going to have Dad take us home," Grace said. "You're coming back home tomorrow, right?"

"That's what my doctors said," Jordan said, recalling Wyatt and Jace's argument about it.

Braxton smiled. "Good. It's been quite lonely at school without you. James, Theodore, and Henry even miss you."

Jordan smiled. *I can't wait to go back home, get back into school, and have my life be normal again. I miss not being with Grace and my friends.*

After they left, Jordan again fell into a calm, dreamless sleep.

CHAPTER 26

Tapping his desk impatiently, Dr. Adrian looked at the dark computer screen. He was supposed to receive a call from one of the men he'd sent to find Jordan and bring him back.

What's taking you so long to contact me, Faustino Benson?

Dr. Adrian angrily looked out his dark window.

Grant walked into Dr. Adrian's office, his brow furrowed.

"What is it, Grant?" Dr. Adrian asked angrily.

"Faustino Benson was killed last night," Grant said, sitting in one of the chairs in front of Dr. Adrian's desk. "His heartbeat stopped, and his chip just sent us a message, alerting us to the sad death of our friend. Could he have found Jordan and Jordan killed him?"

"That's the only likely thing," Dr. Adrian said, watching the video feeds on one of his other computers. "Jordan knows to kill whenever he knows he's being tracked. Did the chip say how Faustino was killed?"

"By a throwing knife," Grant said, looking at the tablet he'd brought with him.

"I guess Jordan knows more than I taught him after all. He must have stabbed Faustino, and Faustino bled to death."

"That's what the records say," Grant reported. "The knife went all the way through Faustino's arm."

"How did Jordan do that? A throwing knife should get lodged, not go all the way through."

"He's clearly learned more than you think these past few years."

"Clearly he has!" Dr. Adrian yelled.

"Sir, you must calm down. If Thurgood is getting you angry now, imagine how much more yelling you'll be doing later in this war," Grant said calmly.

"You're right, Grant. I shouldn't lose my cool. I need to stay focused. If Thurgood is going to do this to everyone I send after him, we're going to lose too many people."

Nodding, Grant got up and walked out of the room.

I guess I'll have to get inside his head to understand what he's planning, where he's located, and who he's in contact with.

Dr. Adrian walked down a hallway and entered one of the labs.

"Ah, Dr. Adrian! So happy you could make it to my lab," Carlos said, walking up to him.

"Yes, yes. Now, please tell me you have that special liquid I asked for?"

"Of course I do! I found all the ingredients myself," Carlos boasted.

"Well, could you get it for me, then?" Dr. Adrian asked impatiently.

"Oh, yes, of course, Dr. Adrian. It would be my pleasure."

The scientist rushed to his office and Dr. Adrian followed him. The room was cluttered with lab equipment, newspapers, test results, and parts for machines.

Looks like he doesn't know how to clean things up properly.

"Sorry about the mess, Dr. Adrian. I just finished an experiment and was going to show the others, but then you arrived."

"Oh, that's all right," Dr. Adrian said, fake-smiling. "I should've told you I was coming."

After a few more minutes of bustling, the scientist finally found the bottle. "Here's the liquid you asked for, Dr. Adrian," he said, handing over the bottle.

Dr. Adrian walked briskly to his office, liquid in hand.

Dr. Adrian read the instructions on the bottle and then pulled off the lid and took a small sip. The liquid smelled like rotten eggs and tasted like burnt fish. Gagging, he carefully set down the bottle.

The room started to sway. Dr. Adrian felt like throwing up and his head hurt. Clutching his head, he sat on the floor, which helped.

That's when the liquid must have started working, because now he could see into Jordan's mind. For a moment, Dr. Adrian was shocked, but then he started digging through Jordan's few memories.

No, not this one—or this one—or that one—aha, here we go!

The memory he was looking for was very recent. It was the one where Jordan killed Faustino Benson.

The memory played back and Dr. Adrian intently watched what had happened to his most faithful companion.

Jordan's going to pay for that. He knows how much Faustino meant to me. I did teach him to kill when threatened, but that didn't mean he had to kill my best friend and companion.

Dr. Adrian angrily searched through more of Jordan's memories. However, he didn't find any more useful ones. He couldn't figure out where Jordan was living because the memory was blocked.

Then it dawned on him. *Jordan must have found a way to block me out.*

Dr. Adrian cursed underneath his breath. Jordan had beaten him in that round, but he wouldn't beat him in the next one.

I need a new idea. Something that'll overpower him so I can find out where he is and catch him.

Before long, an idea did come to Dr. Adrian's mind.

CHAPTER 27

Jordan bolted upright in his bed, panting and sweating. He sensed that someone had recently been inside his mind. He could think of only one person who could possibly do that.

Adrian knows I killed Faustino Benson. Now he knows some of my memories and secrets. I'm surprised my subconscious could overpower him enough to block him out.

Jordan glanced over at his alarm clock. *It's only six in the morning?*

He sat up, looking around his dark room. The sun was starting to peek through the curtains, making his room a bit brighter.

Jordan grabbed his phone from the nightstand and looked at the date. Today was the exact day seven years ago when his and Grace's parents were murdered.

A pang of guilt went through him. He had never told Grace why he was so adamant about finding her and what he'd been doing all these years away from her. *I'm such an idiot. How could I have forgotten to tell her about our parents? That's crucial information I needed to tell her!*

Jordan was angry at himself for not telling her why he was mad at the world, why he was so secretive, why he always had to lie, why he'd ended up in the hospital, and—if she'd already read his background file—why he'd left out a lot of information.

Jordan turned on the TV and the news came on. He was about to change the channel, but then his eye caught the news ticker: "Adrian Corporation is expanding to Egypt."

Egypt, huh? That's a new one. I thought he'd stop expanding after he achieved his fame in Texas.

Jordan's phone buzzed in his lap. It was a text from an unknown number: "You better not screw up my corporate expansion in Egypt or you'll pay the price. I already know your secrets and where you're located. Don't make me do something you'll regret. I know you found the girl I've been after for years and years."

Jordan's blood turned cold.

How did Adrian get my number? I only gave it to a few trusted people. And my cell phone isn't even registered in my name.

Jordan looked back up at the TV, a sense of hopeless washing over him. He knew he could stop the plan from happening, but at what cost?

He snapped out of his thoughts when he heard a knock on the closed door.

"Jordan, can I come in?" a voice asked.

"Sure," Jordan said, sitting up.

Levi opened the door softly and walked in, closing the door behind him. "I heard the TV on, so I decided to see if you were up."

"I've been up since, like, six. I decided to watch some TV, but that just made things worse."

Levi raised an eyebrow. "What do you mean?"

Jordan sighed. "What do you remember me telling you?"

"I don't think you've ever told me anything that happened to your past, other than what was written in your file. Of course, I know some of that isn't true. But you also close yourself off from those around you, and I don't understand why."

Jordan looked down at his lap.

"Jordan, I know you don't like talking about your past. But I need to know why you're scared of everyone. I see how you interact with Grace, Braxton, Henry, and the others. They're the very few people you can be yourself around. But you don't tell me what's going on in your life. I want to help you, but you need to let me inside your emotional barrier."

Jordan looked up, tears welling in his eyes. "The problem is, Dad, I don't know how to let that barrier down. I've had it up for so long that I don't know how to escape it or let anything inside. Even Grace and the guys don't know the true me. The only person who's seen the actual true me is gone."

Levi looked up, concern in his eyes. "Who do you mean?"

"The girl I love. I haven't seen her in years. She was captured by an evil man. I'm part of a rebellion to stop an evil corporation that's now expanding to Egypt. The headmaster of a school I attended called the Academy of Spies taught me all I needed to know and more. I was the top of my class. When the headmaster thought I was ready, he sent me on my first mission to get closer to the man who started the evil corporation. That didn't pan out because some of his henchmen found out my identity. They beat me up and kidnapped me. Little did the headmaster know, that this evil guy would turn me into a mutant and use me for experiments. He also used me as an example to show his workers what he'd do to them if they disobeyed. Since I escaped from him, I've been on the run. I've never returned to the Academy."

"What's this girl's name?" Levi asked.

"Emma," Jordan said sadly, tears spilling from his eyes. He looked down, ashamed about what he'd just told Levi. His hair fell into his eyes.

Levi wrapped an arm around Jordan and pulled him into an embrace. "I'm sorry for what you've gone through. I now understand why you're afraid. You're worried someone else is going to hurt you again. You've been scarred not only physically, but also emotionally, socially, and intellectually. You've probably never told anybody else about all this. You've gone through some pretty tough stuff just to find your sister. You have my respect, and you have Henry's, Theodore's, James's, Braxton's, and Grace's. When people get to know you, they'll have the same respect for you."

Jordan looked up, tears streaking down his face. His dad was crying as well. "It feels good to tell someone what's been on my chest for so long. I forgot what it's like to have someone I can trust and talk to."

"Jordan, it's going to be okay," Levi whispered. "We'll get through this together."

Jordan nodded, more tears falling down his face.

They sat there hugging each other for some time before there was another knock on the door.

Jordan hurriedly brushed away the tears. "Come in," he called.

Grace and Braxton entered, and Grace had a newspaper in her hands. "Dad, Jordan, you need to read this," she said, her voice urgent.

Taking the paper, Jordan immediately saw the bold headline: "Big reward for capture of Jordan Thurgood." After reading it twice, he asked, "Who's placed this supposed reward on my head?"

"Read the article," Grace said sadly, looking at Jordan. "It'll tell you."

> *Dr. Adrian, the CEO of Adrian Corporation, told the press last night that Jordan Thurgood, the runaway juvenile delinquent, has stolen valuable information for a new product Adrian scientists are developing. Dr. Adrian doesn't know how Thurgood got past all the company's security precautions, but claims that he did.*
>
> *Jordan Thurgood is making a name for himself as he steals from all over the United States. He's bounced from Texas to Florida, Montana, California, and finally to Idaho. Police are still wondering how he can get past security when he boards planes; they believe he uses many different disguises.*
>
> *Thurgood was last seen in Boise, Idaho, and recent sightings suggest he's still here in Boise. Police are after him and will bring him back to Dr. Adrian. But if the police can't catch him within a certain amount of time, they will open this search to the public nationwide.*
>
> *Dr. Adrian has currently set the reward at $10,000 for information leading to Thurgood's whereabouts. Clearly Thurgood stole some important and valuable things from Dr. Adrian. Police Chief Grant says that he and his team are getting closer to finding Jordan Thurgood.*

Jordan set down the newspaper in dismay. His dismay then turned into anger. "He's throwing false accusations at me, just so people will be more alert and try to catch me and bring me back to him. Then he'll torture me for the information I hold that'll help me defeat him. He wants the information I have about the Academy, the headmaster, and my friends."

"Could there be a different Jordan Thurgood out there?" Levi asked.

"Thurgood is a common last name, but it sounds like Dr. Adrian and Grant know which Thurgood they're looking for. But it doesn't matter, because I took your last name when you adopted me. It's in the records at the Boise government, but Dr. Adrian doesn't know that."

"So, this news article is just a way to get more people after you?" Braxton asked, looking at Jordan.

Jordan nodded, but still felt confused about something. "How did Dr. Adrian know I went to California? I've never shared where I went. Boise, I understand, because he sent someone after me here at the hospital. And Montana—it doesn't matter why I was in Montana. But California is where the Academy is, and I never shared that I was going back to the Academy with anybody, other than a few guys from that school—" Jordan suddenly stopped talking.

"What is it, Jordan?" Grace asked, growing concerned for her brother.

"I just remembered, Dr. Adrian put a tracking device in me, but I cut it out myself. But then a few years later, he sends someone after me. There could be another tracker in me that I don't know about."

"Why do you think that?" Grace asked, sitting on the ground in front of Jordan's bed.

"Because I remember one day, when I woke up, I felt a stinging sensation in one part of my body, and I just thought I'd worked out too hard the day before. But now that I think more about it, Dr. Adrian must have had another tracker injected into me. The bad thing is, I don't know where it is."

"How do we find it?" Levi asked with determination.

"You don't, unless you have a super strong and powerful scanner," Jordan replied.

"I don't think anybody has that," Braxton stated.

Jordan smiled. "How do you know that?"

Grace, Braxton, and Levi raised their eyebrows and looked confused. Levi asked, "What do you mean? Do you know someone who has a scanner like that?"

"I'm the one who actually made it, but it's all the way in California at the Academy."

"Wait, so you're telling us that you're some sort of super genius?" Braxton asked.

"Yes, that's basically what I'm telling you. Most of the technology that Adrian Corporation has is stuff I've invented, made blueprints for, or started building before I left. They just take the credit for it or claim one of their scientists invented it. They never give me credit for the things I created. In my spare time back then, I was always either fighting with some of the guards who were willing to take me on, inventing, or writing."

"If you were inventing at Adrian Corporation, then why is that scanner in California?" Grace asked.

"Before I went on the mission the headmaster gave me, I was actually inventing even then. The first thing I invented was that scanner. The Academy still uses it to this day."

"And you need to go to California?" Levi asked.

"Yes, but I can't even leave Boise, thanks to that article,

unless . . ." Jordan trailed off.

"Unless what?" Braxton asked.

"I'm not going to finish what I was going to say, because it could get you three mixed up in this mess," Jordan said.

"Tell us, and if we think it's too risky for us, we'll tell you you're on your own," Grace said confidently.

Sighing, Jordan thought about it for a moment. "Fine. What I was going to say was, the guys I went to school with are here in Boise as well. We could all go to California to find that scanner, get me scanned, and then take out the tracking device."

"That's the craziest plan I've ever heard," Grace said, looking at her two older brothers and then at her dad. "But what other choice do we have?"

Levi was lost in his thoughts for a moment before saying, "I agree with Grace. It's a crazy plan, but what other options do we have? We can't let the police catch you and bring you back to Dr. Adrian. You need to finish what you started and have been trying to accomplish for years."

"I'm with you till the end," Braxton said, sounding determined.

Jordan smiled. "Thanks, you three. This really means a lot to me. I just have to let the other guys know what the plan is. Hopefully they'll agree."

CHAPTER 28

"So, you're saying you want us to go with you, your sister, your brother, and your dad to the Academy?" Jace asked on the Zoom call Jordan had set up. In the house they'd bought together, Wyatt and Jace were sitting at the kitchen counter.

"Yes, that's literally what I just said," Jordan said, rolling his eyes.

"And what's this for?" Wyatt asked, reaching for a piece of paper, but struggling to find a pen. Jace chuckled to himself as he watched.

They saw Jordan slap his own face in exasperation. "I need to get back to the Academy and find the scanner I made so I can scan myself and see if Dr. Adrian is still tracking me."

"Oh," Wyatt said. "Why didn't you just say that before?"

"I said it to you guys like fifty times!"

"I guess we didn't hear you," Jace said sincerely.

"Okay, before I go punch a wall or break something else, are you guys coming or not?" Jordan asked.

"Of course we're coming!" Jace and Wyatt said at the same time.

Jordan paused for a moment. "You guys do realize you'll be risking your lives again? Just like the old days."

"Yes," Wyatt said. "It's what we live for. We live for the excitement and thrill of nearly dying and getting caught."

"If I didn't know you usually act like this, I'd ask if you were on something again," Jordan said, smirking.

"What?" Jace asked, looking at Wyatt.

"Do you remember when Wyatt drank that mysterious bottle that appeared on his bed one day?" Jordan asked, trying not to laugh. "We both told him not to drink it because we didn't know what was in it, and what did he do? He drank it. He got so high on whatever was in that thing that we couldn't get him to stop talking. He was saying the most random stuff. And then we met with the headmaster, and Wyatt just babbled about pink bunnies, rainbows, how he's super clumsy, how he ate your secret candy stash, and a bunch of other random stuff."

"That did not happen!" Wyatt said defensively, his face growing red.

"Yes, it did, Wyatt," Jace laughed.

"How do I not remember it, then?" Wyatt asked, scrunching up his nose and looking confused.

"Because you were so high on whatever was in that bottle!" Jace exclaimed, shaking his head.

"Oh."

"Anyway," Jordan said, still laughing. "Plan on getting a text or call from me sometime this week. Be prepared."

"Will do," Jace said.

After they hung up, Wyatt said, "I was not high."

"Oh, yes, you were," Jace said, smiling.

"Do you have any proof?" Wyatt asked, raising an eyebrow.

"A video on my phone," Jace said, grinning.

"Uh, I don't want to watch it. I really don't want to know what I said," Wyatt said, stepping away from the counter.

Jace laughed.

Standing in the kitchen later that evening, Jordan stared off into space, lost in his thoughts.

Grace, Braxton, and his dad were already in bed, so he was on his own. He didn't feel like going to bed quite yet.

The only light that was on was above the kitchen sink, and it cast eerie shadows around the kitchen.

I can't believe I'll be on the road again. I feel that's all I've been doing for the past eight years.

Jordan looked at the clock.

Why am I feeling weird? I didn't forget to do anything today. I already did my homework, finished my chores, cleaned up my room, did the dishes, and made sure all the cars are locked and the keys are on their hooks. What could it be, then?

Jordan listened intently for a moment, noticing the house was creaking even more than usual. And there were strange sounds coming from somewhere in the basement.

Something's not right.

Jordan pulled a knife from the sheath of throwing knives attached to a belt loop on his jeans. He held the knife close, ready to throw it. With his other hand, he grabbed the night vision goggles he'd been working on earlier and put them on. Then he walked over to the sink and turned off the light.

Instead of darkness, Jordan saw greenish light. *Let's see if there's anything out of the ordinary going on.* He made his way from the kitchen into the entryway, scanning his surroundings as he went.

Jordan had added a few extra features to his night vision goggles. The goggles showed a notification whenever there was movement, light, or a person nearby. At the touch of a button, the goggles could scan an entire area. He could contact people on his phone from the goggles. Once he programmed additional goggles, he would be able to share what he was seeing with other wearers of the modified goggles.

Sure enough, a few seconds later Jordan received a notification. *Let's see what we found.*

Opening the notification, Jordan saw that several people were positioned outside and inside the house. Fear and worry gripped him.

Who are these people? How did they get into the house? Are these Dr. Adrian's men, sent here to capture me again?

Luckily, none of them had on night vision goggles, from what Jordan could tell. They were all relying on light and sound.

Opening his phone, Jordan typed a group text to Levi, Braxton, and Grace. "Don't move, don't turn on any lights, stay where you are. People are surrounding us. If you do what I say, we might make it out alive."

Jordan pressed up against a wall, waiting for a response. Finally, Braxton texted back, "How do you know?"

Jordan messaged back, "I didn't go to bed when you three went upstairs. I got a strange feeling, so I put on my night vision goggles."

After a few intense moments, a message appeared from Levi. "Glad you were up when they appeared. Do you have your throwing knives on you?"

Smiling to himself, Jordan replied, "Yes, I usually do for just this reason."

"Okay, that's good," Levi messaged back. "I don't have any weapons right now. You think they'll attack?"

Jordan responded, "I think they're waiting for a signal from their commander. If he doesn't see anybody worth attacking, they'll eventually leave. But the commander knows I'm here, so they'll be here for a while."

Grace messaged, "What do you want us to do, then? We could be up all night before they attack."

Jordan thought for a moment. "Scratch my first message. All of you make noise. They won't attack you because you aren't who they're after. As they're distracted, I'll carefully take down each person inside the house. There's a lot of them, though, so it'll be a while before I can get to you guys."

Levi messaged back, "Don't worry about us. Just do whatever you need to get upstairs."

Jordan messaged, "All right. When I signal you, make the biggest distractions you can. For now, pretend you're still asleep, and I'll secure the downstairs."

Time to do what I was trained to do and finally fight back, instead of running away from my problems.

Jordan put his throwing knife back into the sheath and grabbed his dart gun from a different belt loop. Finding his pouch of poison darts, he placed a cartridge into his gun.

All right, let's do this. Jordan walked silently towards his dad's office. He carefully opened the double doors, making sure they didn't creak. He saw two men looking through papers.

Jordan pulled the trigger two times. Two poison darts flew out noiselessly, hitting the men in the chest or neck. They both fell to the floor, not making a sound.

Jordan messaged his family, "Two men down, two still left downstairs. Also one on the stairs and two more upstairs. Watch for my signal for the distraction."

Levi messaged, "Good job so far. We're standing by."

Jordan carefully made his way through the house's main level, shooting darts at one man in the living room and one in the laundry room.

All right, now the stairs need to be cleared of intruders. Once that's done, I'll contact the family.

Jordan heard movement upstairs. Now his scanner showed additional men on the main floor and upper floor. Groaning inwardly, he messaged Grace, Braxton and Levi, "Situation isn't good. More guys coming in from somewhere."

Braxton messaged, "Not good. Does that mean there's less men outside?"

Jordan hurriedly scanned outside the house. Sure enough, there were fewer men outside than before. He messaged, "Brax, you're right. Get out through your bedroom windows. The men outside don't have night vision goggles. Do it now!"

Levi messaged, "What about you? You can't take all those guys. More are probably coming."

Jordan replied, "I have no idea what to do. There are too many."

A sense of panic and dread hit him. *How am I supposed to protect my family and stop these people from coming into the house?*

A strange, unexpected idea came to mind, a new way to use his powers.

After a second of consideration, Jordan knew he either had to follow through with the idea or risk all of them getting caught.

Jordan messaged back, "Okay, I have a crazy plan. I don't know if it will work or not, but I need you guys to get out of the house. When you get across the street, let me know ASAP."

As moments passed, Jordan assumed Braxton, Levi, and Grace were climbing out their bedroom windows. Finally, Levi messaged, "We're all standing across the street."

Jordan took a deep breath, slowly exhaled, and cleared his head of unwanted thoughts.

I know I can do this. I just have to focus.

Guided by his intuition, Jordan stood up straighter, extended his arms before him, and focused all his energy and power into the intruders. He felt himself shaking, but he maintained his focus. He could feel invisible power waves emanating from his hands in all directions and extending beyond the house.

The intruders started screaming all at once.

I need to up the power, or the effects will dwindle and the bad guys won't die.

Jordan's shaking increased and he felt sweat running down his back.

I need to think of the pain I've experienced.

He changed his thoughts to the emotional, mental, and physical pain he had endured for most of his life. He heard the men's screams increase and could feel their pain. Soon, he heard men collapsing around him, but he knew some were still alive.

Just a little longer—I only have to use this power a little longer. I can rest after this is all over. I can go back to living my life when Dr. Adrian is stopped once and for all.

Levi messaged, "All the men out here are down. We can feel a little pain, not enough to harm us."

I just unlocked another power. That's so cool!

Jordan wondered if his other powers were getting stronger, too. But he'd have to test that on a different day. Scanning the house, he found no intruders alive. He messaged, "You can come back in."

A few moments later, he heard a knock. Looking through the peephole, he saw Levi, Braxton, and Grace. He unlocked the door for them.

Turning on the entryway light, Levi gave Jordan a look. "What did you use to kill those guys?"

"Well, I have a new special power," Jordan explained, feeling himself growing weak. "I can inject pain inside people's bodies. I can do it to everyone around me or just a certain group."

"That's a remarkable, but dangerous power," Levi commented. "I hope you won't have to use it again anytime soon."

"I hope I don't ever have to use it again," responded Jordan, feeling out of breath.

Levi nodded gravely. "We need to leave for California tomorrow before more trouble comes."

Jordan couldn't have agreed more.

Waking up on a couch, Jordan felt confused. *Was it only last night all those men were here? What happened to the bodies?*

He then recalled Levi calling the police. When the police

came, Levi explained how these men had broken into the house and Levi had protected his family.

Before long, Levi walked into the living room and sat down on the other couch, not saying anything for a moment.

Why has Levi agreed to be by my side through everything? He was once a normal civilian. And now he's been drawn into this war that was supposed to be between Dr. Adrian and me.

"You probably see me as a freak now," Jordan said, looking at Levi.

"I knew you had unique abilities—just not like *that*. But I don't think you're a freak."

Braxton came into the living room and sat across from Jordan. "When are you planning to go to California?"

"Sometime today, because if those men came here last night, what's stopping more from coming again tonight?" Jordan said.

"I thought you took them all out," his dad pointed out.

"There are always more," said Jordan. "Dr. Adrian has more minions than he knows what to do with."

"Well, that's good to know, so I can be even more on alert than I already am," Braxton commented sarcastically.

A knock sounded, and Levi got up to answer the front door. After a cheerful greeting, he let a woman and two teen boys into the house. The boys looked like twins.

Smiling, Levi said, "Jordan and Braxton, this is Madison, my new girlfriend, and her boys, Colton and Devon. We both thought it'd be good for you all to meet each other." Turning to Madison, he said, "My daughter, Grace, is over at her friend's, but you'll meet her soon."

"Uh, hello?" Jordan said as he stood up, feeling awkward.

Madison said hello back cheerfully, then told him how much of a pleasure it was to finally meet him.

"You four are about the same age, so I'm sure you'll find things in common," said Levi. "While Madison and I talk, how about you guys get to know each other?" The two of them went into Levi's office.

Braxton stood, gave a little wave, and said hello. Then several moments passed uncomfortably.

Finally, one of the boys—for some reason, Jordan felt it was Colton—broke the silence. "It's nice to meet you, Jordan and Braxton."

"Uh, same here, Colton?" Jordan said uncertainly, hoping it was the right name.

The twin gave Jordan a surprised look. "How'd you know I'm Colton? Your dad didn't point to us when he said our names."

Braxton looked over at Jordan with surprise.

"Lucky guess." Jordan shrugged. "You look like you could be a Colton."

Colton laughed.

"Do you guys want to—uh, go upstairs so our parents can talk?" Braxton asked.

"Sure," Colton and Devon both said. They followed Jordan and Braxton up the stairs and into Jordan's room.

I really hope we don't get any more trouble from Dr. Adrian's minions, at least while Colton, Devon, and their mom are here. I don't want to get them mixed up in this. Why did Dad have them come over so soon after the attack last night? Does he think we're safe from being attacked again?

"So, uh, what do you guys do for fun?" Jordan asked, sitting on the floor. Braxton sat down next to him, and the twins sat across.

After a few moments, Devon said, "I like to ride my dirt

bike, draw, rock-climb, play soccer and tennis, and write songs."

"Cool," Jordan said, giving a genuine smile.

Colton replied, "Well, like Devon, I like to dirt-bike, draw, rock-climb, and play soccer, but I also like to swim and play football."

Jordan nodded, and Devon asked, "What about you guys?"

Jordan froze. *What do I like doing for fun?*

Braxton didn't say anything, so Jordan said, "Football, dirt-biking, swimming, and playing guitar."

The two boys seemed genuinely interested in what Jordan was saying about himself.

I like these two. My gut tells me I can trust them with anything.

"Will you play us a song?" Colton asked, glancing over at the guitar Levi had given to Jordan.

Jordan hesitated, but he realized he felt comfortable playing for these guys. "I'll play you one I wrote myself," he said, standing. He grabbed his guitar and took a notebook from his desk.

As Jordan played his guitar, Colton and Devon were silent, looking very impressed.

"You should make a career out of that," Devon said when Jordan finished. "You have raw talent." Colton nodded in agreement.

Jordan's face grew red. "Thanks."

"No problem, Jordan," Colton said, looking sincere. "We only say the truth."

After thinking for a few moments, Jordan said, "So, I've never had a whole lot of friends because I'm always on the run and people tend to use me for their own agendas or personal gain. But with you two, I feel like we all could actually be friends, and I wouldn't have to pretend to be someone I'm not."

Colton and Devon nodded, and Devon said, "Your dad told us you have trouble trusting people and making friends. And we genuinely want to be your friends. We've been used ourselves, so we know what it's like."

Jordan smiled, feeling better. But then he grew serious. "Can I trust you two with something?"

With sober expressions, Colton and Devon both nodded.

I can do this. I just hope I don't hurt anyone when I show Colton and Devon my newest power.

Standing, Jordan solemnly asked, "Could I try something on one of you? It could hurt, but I'll try my best to not exert a lot of it into you. Just a little to show you guys a new trick I learned."

Colton stood. "I'll do it."

"Are you ready?" Jordan asked.

"Ready as I'll ever be," Colton said, shifting from one foot to the other.

I hope I don't hurt him too badly.

Jordan used the power that he'd used on the intruders, but on a much smaller scale.

Colton grunted, growing uncomfortable.

Devon looked worried. "What're you doing to Colton?"

Braxton watched silently, his eyes wide. Jordan could tell he knew what was going on.

"It's the secret I said I was going to show you," said Jordan. "I call it my pinpoint power. If I feel threatened, I can mentally inject pain into people's body. Specifically targeting their weaknesses. If I do too much, I can kill them. Lucky for Colton, I'm not feeling threatened or angry." Smiling, Jordan decreased the pain.

Panting, Colton looked at Jordan. "That's really powerful. Does your dad know?"

"Yeah, he learned about it last night," Jordan admitted.

"According to a news report I recently read, apparently Dr. Adrian claims something top secret was stolen from him and you're the one to blame," said Devon. "Is this power what you stole?"

As Devon stared at him expectantly, Jordan recalled the news article Devon was talking about. "I didn't steal it," Jordan said. "He gave me this power and others, too, and then I escaped."

"So, that's why you've been on the run," Colton said, sitting back down on the ground.

Jordan nodded.

"That's a dangerous secret you've told us, Jordan," Devon said, his piercing green eyes looking directly into Jordan's eyes.

"Like I said, I trust you two."

Colton and Devon nodded.

Jordan wanted to change the subject. Smiling, he clapped his hands together. "So, you guys didn't happen to bring your dirt bikes, did you?"

"Yup, we did," Colton said, grinning. "Wanna go for a ride?"

Colton and Devon unstrapped their bikes from their mom's car, and Jordan and Braxton rolled out the bikes they'd recently bought from a neighbor.

Out on the open road, Jordan tried to enjoy the wind whipping through his hair and clothing. He looked back for a moment, making sure all three were still following him. They'd agreed that Jordan should take the lead.

As he rode, Jordan wondered why he'd said yes to the headmaster and turned his life upside down. He could have spent his teenage years riding around on his dirt bike, having lots of loyal friends, being emotionally stable, trusting people—in short, not being who he was now.

I hope nobody back at home gets attacked while we're away. I don't think I could take the guilt of knowing I wasn't able to help fight back.

Before leaving the house, Jordan had equipped them all with helmet radios. Now he heard some static as one of the other guys tried to contact him.

"Yeah, what's up?" Jordan asked, turning up the volume.

"Do you know where we're going, Jordan?" Braxton asked, his voice crisp and clear through the radio.

"I have no idea," Jordan said. "You ready to go back already?"

"No, it's fine," Colton radioed in.

"Actually, I've seen a field where there's some jumps and stuff," Jordan said.

"Sounds good," said Devon. "Lead on!"

■■■■■■■■■■■■■■■■■■

The boys returned home an hour later, worn out from riding. For the moment, Jordan's worries about more of Dr. Adrian's men coming were dashed away.

"How was it?" Levi asked as they all sat at the kitchen table.

"Really fun," Braxton said.

"We should do it again soon," Jordan added.

"Yeah, we really should," Devon said.

Colton nodded, but couldn't speak because he'd shoved an entire roll into his mouth.

"Man, you've got a big mouth," Jordan said, laughing at Colton.

Colton shot Jordan a look and threw a roll at him.

They all laughed, and Jordan bit into the roll.

"Where's Grace?" Braxton asked, his mouth full of roll.

"Still over at Henry's," Levi responded. He and Madison were seemingly unphased by the roll frenzy.

Using the same singsong voice, Colton and Devon asked in unison, "Who's Henry?"

Jordan and Braxton looked at each other, trying not to laugh at the twins.

Braxton replied, "He's Grace's friend."

Just then, Grace walked into the room. Jordan hadn't heard her enter the house.

"Uh, Dad, could I talk to you for a moment?" she asked. She looked extremely nervous.

"Of course, Grace," Levi said, getting up from the kitchen table.

A few moments later, Grace came back into the kitchen and whispered in Jordan's ear, "Dad wants you in his office."

When Jordan entered the office, his dad was pacing back and forth, looking anxious.

"What's wrong, Dad?" Jordan asked, growing concerned.

"Grace saw more men watching the street when she was walking home from Henry's. There's no way for us to leave for California."

Jordan felt panic well up inside him.

How did they get here so fast?

"I can take down those guys." Jordan clutched the edge of Levi's desk, his knuckles white. "How many did Grace see?"

"About four so far, but there appear to be more coming," Levi said gravely.

Jordan processed this for a moment. "I think I can take them all down in one blow. It'll use a lot of my energy, but at this point, I'll do anything to get to California in one piece."

Levi nodded and then went strangely silent.

"Are you okay?" Jordan asked.

Levi fell to the floor.

What just happened?

Jordan's eyes grew wide as Levi writhed on the floor, his appearance changing. When he stood up again, he didn't look like Levi anymore. Jordan felt fear rush through him.

It can't be him. That's impossible.

"Ah, it's nice to see you again, Jordan," Dr. Adrian said, smiling menacingly.

"What did you do to Levi?" Jordan asked, stepping back from Dr. Adrian.

"That doesn't need to concern you right now, my boy," Dr. Adrian said, stepping closer to Jordan. "What you should be concerned about is yourself. You're surrounded. There's no escape. Either you can come willingly with me, or you can die right here."

He already knows what I'll choose. I don't understand why he's giving me a choice.

Jordan heard glass breaking in the kitchen, followed by a chorus of screams.

Not them. I shouldn't have dragged them into this.

Jordan's fear intensified as he imagined his siblings and his newfound friends being taken away.

"So, what's it going to be, Jordan?" Dr. Adrian asked.

"I would rather die than follow you," Jordan said tensely, moving away from Dr. Adrian.

"It didn't have to come to this, ending your life right now at such a young age, but you're the one that brought it upon yourself," Dr. Adrian said, pulling out a knife.

Do I even have a knife or something to fight back?

Jordan looked for a weapon of some sort. He didn't have anything. The only protection he had was his dirt-biking gear, which he was still wearing.

Dr. Adrian lunged at him, and Jordan jumped to the side.

"Yes, you're right, I'm the one who brought it upon myself, but who says I'm going to die?" Jordan questioned, tripping Dr. Adrian.

As Dr. Adrian hit the ground, the knife fell out of his hand, hitting the ground with a clatter. Jordan hurriedly grabbed it before Dr. Adrian could regain his composure.

"You seem to have gotten more prideful over the years," Dr. Adrian said, pulling out another knife. "But I'm going to break your pride, and then you'll beg me for mercy."

He has another knife on him. I can see the hilt sticking up through his pocket.

Jordan swiped the knife at Dr. Adrian, cutting through his suit sleeve into his forearm.

"You forgot, didn't you," Dr. Adrian said, smiling darkly. "I can't feel pain."

Dr. Adrian's forearm bled freely, blood dripping onto the office's wood floor. But his only focus was on Jordan.

Jordan breathed deeply before lunging at Dr. Adrian again, this time slicing open Dr. Adrian's hand.

"No matter what, Jordan, I'm going to end what you started.

I'll always find you. I'll always capture you. There's no escape from me."

"Your talk is cheap," Jordan said calmly, holding the knife in a defensive position. "Your promises are nothing but lies. I've learned this the hard way, and I'm not gonna let anyone else fall into the same trap I did."

Dr. Adrian came at Jordan, but Jordan blocked the worst of the blow. His hand stung, and he felt blood dripping down his fingertips.

"You've gotten sloppy with your knife fighting," Dr. Adrian said, trying to distract Jordan.

"And you've gotten slower with age," Jordan retorted.

Dr. Adrian lunged on top of Jordan, knocking the knife out of Jordan's hand.

Jordan looked in fear at Dr. Adrian. *This isn't good. I'm not experienced enough to use my pinpoint power while fighting someone. I can't pause long enough to clear my head.*

Dr. Adrian put his own knife to Jordan's throat and used his other hand to grab the fallen knife.

"You are going to die," Dr. Adrian whispered intensely, digging the knife deeper into Jordan's throat.

Jordan felt blood dripping down the side of his neck. *He can kill me if he wants. He can end this war. The war I was unwillingly dragged into.*

Dr. Adrian then pressed the other knife into Jordan's chest, grinning madly as Jordan winced in pain.

"I have finally beaten you," Dr. Adrian said, digging both knives deeper into Jordan's body.

Choking on blood rushing up his throat, Jordan spat some in Dr. Adrian's face. *If I die now, it might as well be heroic and for a good cause.*

Dr. Adrian punched Jordan hard in the face, then pushed the knives deeper.

Jordan started to shake and continued to gag, sweat rolling down his face.

"Now there's nothing stopping you from taking over the world, Adrian," Jordan choked, feeling himself fading.

Dr. Adrian smiled darkly. "Oh, I know this, Jordan. And with you out of the way, dying on this floor, nobody's going to stop

me. Not even that pathetic school you came from."

Dr. Adrian ripped the dog-tag necklace from Jordan's neck and then got up and walked out of the room.

He can take those dog tags. He won't be able to do anything with them.

Jordan's breathing became shallower and shallower as he continued to lose more blood. *At least I'm being put out of my misery. I know my life was a waste of time, but at least I'll die a hero and know I helped all I could.*

Jordan's body shut down. And eventually his mind shut down, too, with most of his blood on the floor.

CHAPTER 29

Sitting in darkness in a speeding van, Grace had no idea what was going on or what was going to happen to her.

Braxton, Colton, and Devon were right across from her. She couldn't see them, but she knew they were there. Madison and Levi were on either side of her.

"What do you think's going to happen to us?" Braxton asked worriedly.

"We'll probably face the same fate Jordan did when he first met Dr. Adrian," Levi responded.

Grace stared blankly into the darkness. She knew what Dr. Adrian would do to Jordan if he caught him. *I hope Adrian didn't kill him.*

"Hopefully Jordan got away and he's coming for us," Colton said with a tinge of confidence.

Grace somehow knew that Jordan wasn't coming to save them.

"What if he doesn't come?" Braxton asked. "What are we going to do then?"

Madison spoke up for the first time since they'd been caught. "Well, we'll fight our own way out of torture town and then find out where Jordan went and what happened to him, if he isn't dead already or isn't being killed as we speak."

"Well, you're looking at this very brightly," Colton said sarcastically.

"You're welcome, son," Madison retorted. "Someone at least needs to state the obvious."

"Now's not the time to be saying stuff like that," scolded Levi.

"Sorry, dear," Madison said, sounding sincere.

I hope Jordan is okay.

Grace didn't know how long they were in the van because she couldn't see her watch and didn't have her phone.

The van stopped.

It's never a good sign if the van you're being held captive in just stopped moving.

When two men opened the doors, Grace shielded her eyes from the sun. As she stepped from the van, she saw guards all around.

"I'm very sorry for the inconvenience, but I needed to talk to your son," a voice said.

Turning around, Grace saw a tall, lanky man walking towards them. She somehow knew he was Dr. Adrian, the man Jordan had told them so many disturbing things about. He had black hair with white streaks, and his eyes were black. His skin was pale, as if he'd never been in the sun.

"What did you do to my son?" Levi asked.

"Who are you asking about? Jordan? Oh, he died," the man said simply, showing no emotion.

"He can't be dead!" cried Braxton as tears welled up in his eyes.

That's impossible. Grace felt numb with shock. "I don't believe you," she said defiantly, feeling proud of herself for speaking up.

The man raised an eyebrow. "You don't believe me?"

"Jordan is better at fighting than anyone I know," Grace said. "He's never been beaten."

"Is this proof enough?" the man asked, holding up Jordan's dog-tag necklace, which was covered in dried blood.

Grace gasped. The necklace was indeed Jordan's. She knew he never took it off.

"Why did you kill him?" Colton questioned.

"His time of living was expiring soon, anyway," the man said, shrugging. "He's always been my greatest opponent. It was only a matter of time before he was exterminated."

Colton clenched his jaw in silent anger.

"Now that you've all faced the truth about Jordan, let me introduce myself," the man said curtly.

"You're Dr. Adrian," Grace spat.

"I'm surprised Jordan told you about me," Dr. Adrian said, looking mildly surprised.

"Jordan's been very open with us," Levi said, glaring at Dr. Adrian. "But you've kept secrets from him. For example, not telling him about his powers."

"I didn't think he deserved to know," Dr. Adrian said.

"You're lying," Grace pointed out, smirking.

Dr. Adrian's smile faded. "My, this girl is smart. I might have to keep her around."

The only way I'll ever cooperate with him is over my dead body.

Grace glared at Dr. Adrian. His eyes were black holes that would suck in life and never let it back out. *Jordan warned me about this monster and what he would do to me. Where is my brother when I need him?*

"She isn't an object you can tweak and try to fix," Braxton said, stepping forward to stand next to Grace. "None of us will ever help with whatever sick work you're doing."

Dr. Adrian looked at Grace. "Do you believe you can make a difference in the world, Grace?"

"Yes, but the way you're doing it isn't right," Grace said, angrily spitting out each word.

I have never hated anyone as much as I hate Dr. Adrian. Why does he think what he's doing is good? How does the government not know about this?

"Do you want powers like your brother?" Dr. Adrian asked, flashing a sinister grin.

Grace's blood turned ice cold. *He knows as well as I do that Jordan's the only one who's ever survived those tests.* She didn't want to experience what Jordan had to endure. Dr. Adrian made it sound like he was going to change the world in a good way, but in reality he wanted to use people as weapons.

"No, I do *not* want powers like Jordan," Grace said. "He told me all about the process and how painful it was to endure what you put him through. He's still in pain sometimes."

Dr. Adrian looked taken aback, but quickly regained his composure.

How did Jordan survive this man? I don't know how long I'll be able to survive. I'm willing to stall long enough for Jordan to come, but how long will that be? What will I have to endure so Jordan has enough time to follow the trail and find us?

Grace and her family were led inside and put in separate cells to await their fates. Fear tore her inside as she paced her cell anxiously. Hearing distant screams, she hoped none of her family was hurt.

Where is Jordan when you need him? How did he cope with all the fear and anxiety of being here?

Staring at one of the cell walls, Grace noticed a small slot. She slid in her fingers and felt some sort of book. As she carefully pulled out a well-worn notebook, she saw that it had Jordan's name on it.

She opened the notebook to the first page. Sure enough, it was Jordan's handwriting.

> *To anyone lucky enough to find this—*
>
> *You have been caught by Dr. Adrian, but hopefully you won't face the same fate I did. If you know who I am, then you know that my fate has been planned and what I've had to endure was supposed to happen. You know that I must save the world from utter destruction by the man who captured you.*
>
> *I want to give you some vital information. I may sound crazy to people who don't know me or understand who I am and perhaps even to people who know me. I am much more than anyone can imagine. The powers I possess have given me great talents and great abilities to do good, but they could have*

major consequences for me and everyone else if I don't control them. The powers I hold are dangerous and can kill anybody, perhaps even myself. I have hurt myself trying to figure out these powers, but I've also had visions about them. The work I've done to get this far in life has been tough on my mental, emotional, and physical well-being.

I've been hurt countless times by the man who has captured you. I still fear Dr. Adrian to this day. I cannot describe all the torture I've had to experience. I write to you, whoever is reading this, some encouraging words so you can survive whatever Dr. Adrian throws your way. Don't give up hope. I promise that I will come when the time is right and save you. Hope is what brings Dr. Adrian down. Do not be afraid of whatever happens to you. I know the anxiety you feel because I have experienced it firsthand.

You are here in this cell for reasons I do not entirely know.

I must stop writing for now, for reasons you do not need to know. I left you some blank pages to write on. I hope my words have helped you feel like you can deal with anything that happens to you here in this sinister building.

—Jordan

Grace finished reading her brother's first entry, quite surprised at how well written it was.

She was going to be strong like her brother. Feeling her fears and anxiety subsiding, she inspected the cell, but found nothing further. She felt grateful to have a book from her brother that she could read. It made her feel closer to him than ever before.

Grace carefully replaced the book and sat down on the worn-out sleeping mat.

I hope sooner or later you come for us, Jordan. If you have the powers to read my thoughts, I hope you know that I'm willing to put up with all the pain Dr. Adrian puts me through so you can defeat him when the time is right.

Feeling exhausted from the long day, Grace fell asleep with new hope and new courage.

CHAPTER 30

Jordan gasped, feeling sharp pain in his neck and chest.

I died. I remember slipping away with Dr. Adrian standing above me, and yet I'm still alive. Do I have a healing power, perhaps?

He found himself still lying on the floor of Levi's office in a crusty pool of his own blood. Before trying to sit up, he inspected the wounds in his side. Then he winced in pain as he got up on his feet. Shakily walking to the door, he saw a wall clock and realized what day it was.

I've been dead for five days?! My family has been kidnapped for five days. Dr. Adrian has had five days to do whatever kind of torture he wants.

Jordan pushed the worries aside and focused on the task at hand. He had to find out where Dr. Adrian was keeping his family and get there as fast as he could before Dr. Adrian did them any more harm.

With an awful taste of bile in his mouth, Jordan walked to

the kitchen and got a glass of water. Then he walked through the house, looking for clues of where his family could have been taken. Except for some broken dishes in the kitchen, everything seemed to be in its proper place.

I should call Jace and Wyatt and see if they've been caught by Dr. Adrian.

Jordan went up to his bedroom and grabbed his phone from its charger. He saw several missed calls from Jace. He called Jace, and Jace answered right after the first ring.

"Why haven't you been answering my calls?" Jace asked.

"Well, I kind of came back from the dead," Jordan said, a smile in his voice.

"You—I'm sorry, what?" Jace asked incredulously, his tone changing from panic to confusion.

"You remember my powers I told you about?" Jordan asked.

"Yeah, how could I forget something like that?" Jace said.

"Okay, well, apparently one of my new powers that I didn't even know I had is healing. Don't ask me how I found that out. But anyway, I came back from the dead."

"Someone killed you?" Jace asked, his voice growing alarmed.

"Well . . ." Jordan knew he had to tell Jace now. "Yes, someone killed me. That someone was Dr. Adrian. He tracked me down, killed me, then kidnapped my family. I have no idea where he's keeping them. Probably in one of his many buildings."

I hope Jace doesn't think I'm delusional or something.

"I thought you got rid of all the trackers Dr. Adrian's scientists put in you," Wyatt said, butting into the conversation.

"Apparently not all of them. Instead of kidnapping me, Dr.

Adrian thought it would be a great idea to kill me. But little does he know that I came back from the dead, just to annoy him even more."

Jace and Wyatt were quiet for a moment. Then Wyatt asked, "You need to go to California, don't you?"

"Yes, I do, Wyatt. The Academy's the only place I know of that has a powerful scanner." Jordan paused. "At least, I hope it's still there. I'm not entirely sure. All that I know is I have to go to the Academy."

"Does your dad know about your California plan?" Jace asked wryly.

"Yes, he does." Jordan rubbed a hand over his face. "We were supposed to leave four days ago, but Dr. Adrian changed those plans."

"So, Levi's going to help you get to California?" Wyatt asked.

"Yes, with Grace, Braxton, Levi's girlfriend, and her two sons. They all sounded willing to help."

"Oh, that's good to hear," Jace said.

"Now I need to go search for my family, but I have no idea where to start."

"We'll be over soon with the rest of the group," Wyatt said in a calming voice. "We'll make a plan together. Gather all your weapons, gadgets, and anything else you'll need for the trip."

Jordan sighed. "Okay, if you insist on coming, I won't stop you. But you do realize you're risking your lives for me again? I could just solo this mission on my own."

"We all knew we'd be risking our lives when we agreed to take on any challenge," Wyatt said stubbornly. "And this is for a good cause."

Jordan heard Jace agree. He tried his best not to smile about his friends, but he couldn't help it. "All right, fine, I give in. Meet me at my dad's house in a few hours. Bring the rest of the gang."

"Will do!" Jace said.

What have I gotten my friends into now? They're surely going to die. But I don't have much choice now because I already agreed to let them come.

Around one o'clock, Jordan's friends started arriving. Soon, he had his gang back together, including Jace, Wyatt, Henry, James, and Theodore. Three of Jordan's other friend's also came, Oliver, Nate, and Lucas. All three had attended the Academy, but didn't know about Jordan's powers. That was something Jordan would tell them on a different day, when they weren't starting a rescue mission.

"So, why are we here?" Lucas asked. A couple months older than Jordan, Lucas had straight, jet-black hair and cold, hazel eyes.

"Well, you guys do know my family has been kidnapped, right?" Jordan asked, raising an eyebrow.

"Yeah, but that doesn't explain why we're here," Oliver said, sitting down at the table next to Lucas. Oliver was seventeen, a year older than Jordan. He had dirty-blond hair that was slightly curly on top, and his eyes were brown.

"I need your help finding and saving them," Jordan explained. "I couldn't ask anybody else because they'd just think I'm crazy."

"Oh, why couldn't you have said that in the first place?" Nate asked. He shared the same birthday with Jordan and Grace. He had green eyes and dark-brown hair.

"I'm not the one who contacted you guys," Jordan said. "Jace and Wyatt did."

"That explains a lot," Oliver said, glaring over at Jace and Wyatt, who glared back.

Here comes the fighting. "I'll give you the rundown of what's been going on," Jordan quickly said. "Dr. Adrian somehow found me here, kidnapped my family, and killed me. But instead of dying, I magically healed myself. Today's actually the first time I've been awake in five days."

Having already heard about the healing, Jace and Wyatt didn't look phased, but the other boys were all incredulous.

"What could've healed you?" Oliver asked, leaning forward in his chair.

"Well, it's one of the powers I've developed over the years," Jordan explained. "I've never gotten killed before, so I never knew I had this power until today."

"That is so cool," Lucas said, playing with the dog tags around his neck. All six of the boys who'd attended the Academy wore them.

"Yeah, it's pretty cool," Jordan said. "But let's not dwell on it. Other peoples' lives are at stake here. If we don't plan fast, they could end up dead before we even get there."

"How are we even going to know where they're located?" Henry asked, his eyes bloodshot. Grace's kidnapping was clearly taking a toll on him.

Jordan smiled. "Dr. Adrian took my dog tags, not only my Academy ones, but also the ones my parents gave me. Little did he know, I installed a tracker in case I ever lost them."

Nate's face grew brighter as he smiled. "Good job, Jordan! You and your amazing tech always get us out of the toughest spots."

"Thanks for the compliment, Nate," Jordan said as he pulled up his tracker software on his laptop. It took him a minute to scroll through all his trackers. "They're in Montana," he finally said, looking up from the screen.

Dread consumed him.

"They're in Montana?" Theodore asked, sounding surprised.

"I thought it would be somewhere with lots of people," Oliver said, mostly to himself.

"Dr. Adrian's corporation is all over the world, Oliver," said Lucas. "He's opening a building in Egypt soon."

"Thanks for telling me the news, Lucas," Oliver said coldly to his friend.

"Anyways," Jordan said, directing attention away from his two friends. "The problem isn't about getting to Montana. It's about getting into the building. The security in that place is very tight and very secure. It'll take all our effort to get into the building. But now we at least know where my family is. I say we leave here early tomorrow and make our way to Montana. For now, prepare yourselves the best you can. Gather whatever you need. Tomorrow we won't have time."

"We really are doing this," James breathed out, looking scared.

Jordan felt a pang of empathy for James. At one point, Jordan had been scared to go into the unknown, not knowing if he'd survive another day. But since he'd been in death's pathway so many times and had to risk his life more than once, now he never had to worry about being scared to go into the unknown. But James had never gone on a mission like this. The only reason he was here was because Jordan wanted to bring along his closest friends. He'd felt surprised when James had agreed the second Jordan asked him.

As James walked to the living room, Jordan stopped him. "James, do you really want to come with me? You don't have to."

James shook his head. "I'm not going to let my friends get killed without me being there. Besides, it'll be a great story to tell people. This is a once-in-a-lifetime opportunity I couldn't refuse. Don't think I don't know what could happen on this rescue mission."

Jordan nodded. "I'm glad. I couldn't have asked for a better man on my team."

That night, Jordan lay awake in his bed. His friends were all sleeping downstairs in the living room. They'd all gone to bed before Jordan even went upstairs.

He looked up at the ceiling, listening to the silence of the house. Nobody was up, as far as Jordan knew.

I guess I really am going to Montana again. I thought I'd never have to go back there.

Jordan looked over at his alarm clock. It was only eleven o'clock.

Why can't I sleep? I'm not usually this tense before a mission.

Jordan shook his head and pressed the palms of his hands on his eyes, hoping sleep would overcome him at any moment, but that didn't happen.

I'm going to check on everyone to see if they're okay.

Jordan quietly got out of bed and walked downstairs in his boxers, not caring about putting on a shirt or pants.

Pausing on the landing halfway down, he listened for a moment. He heard only snores from the living room.

Jordan finished walking down the stairs and peered into the living room, making sure everyone was in the room. Sure enough, they all were there.

At least they've fallen asleep. That's all that matters. I can find time to sleep later.

Jordan walked into the kitchen and sat at the table, feeling his hands slightly shaking. After listening to his friends snoring for a moment, he got back up, went over to the pantry, and took out a bag of chips. He returned to the table and began eating the chips as quietly as possible.

Before long, he heard the footsteps of someone coming into the kitchen. When he turned, he saw Wyatt standing in his boxers.

"I thought you'd be up," Wyatt whispered as he pulled up a chair next to Jordan.

"Was I *that* loud?" Jordan whispered back.

"No, but I could tell by your face that you weren't likely to fall asleep tonight," Wyatt explained.

"Oh."

"Are you okay, Jordan?" Wyatt quietly asked.

"No, I'm not. I nearly died when I tried escaping Montana the first time, and now I'm afraid I'll get you and the others killed if I make the wrong move or call the wrong shot. It's a lot of pressure on me. I haven't led a group of people in a long time."

Wyatt was silent for a moment. "It's going to be okay, Jordan. We're all here to help you."

Jordan nodded. "We'll need all the strength we can get."

CHAPTER 31

With her back to her cell door, Grace tried to get comfortable on her sleeping mat.

How many other prisoners in here has Dr. Adrian kidnapped from their homes?

Grace heard another scream from somewhere inside the building.

So far, Dr. Adrian's guards had not come to get her for torture or anything else harmful. They had come to her cell only to give her food and water.

I guess Dr. Adrian is still planning what he's going to do with me.

She had read some more of the book Jordan had left in her cell, but she was tired of reading so she thought she could try to sleep. But sleep wasn't coming.

Sometime later, the lock on her door hissed open and two guards came walking into the cell.

"Dr. Adrian would like to speak with you privately," the

guard on the right said to Grace.

"Okay," Grace said, feeling uncertain.

Surrounded by guards, she walked down the hallway to an elevator.

What's going to happen to me when I face Dr. Adrian? What will happen to my family?

After the elevator ride, the guards remained silent as they walked her down a long hallway and into a pristine office lobby.

This must be Dr. Adrian's office.

The secretary looked up from her computer and talked quietly with one of the guards, then pressed a button on her desk.

"Miss Grace," she said, "Dr. Adrian will see you now."

The secretary's voice was monotone and bore no emotion. She wasn't a pretty lady, either. She wore a grey jumpsuit, had long, red, curly hair, wore glasses low on the bridge of her nose, and had pale skin like Dr. Adrian's.

Still silent, the guards escorted Grace to the door on the far left. One guard knocked on the door and then opened it.

Dr. Adrian looked up from one of the computers on his desk, slightly smiling at Grace. "You all may go," he said to the guards. "Grace isn't a threat to me."

The guards nodded, saluted Dr. Adrian, and then filed out of the room, the last guard closing the door behind him.

Returning his attention to Grace, Dr. Adrian gestured for her to sit in one of the chairs in front of his desk.

I guess I better do what he wants for now, until I figure out a plan.

Grace sat, feeling tense and fearful. After a few moments of intense silence, Dr. Adrian said, "You are much more patient than Jordan was. That's what I like about you. Do you know why I haven't hurt you or your family, Grace?"

Grace thought for a moment. "No, I don't know why."

"It's because you and your family aren't threats to me. Your brother was, yes, but he's been eliminated from the picture. You and your family are here so you guys don't get hurt. You are all safe here. Out there, you and your family won't be safe."

She didn't believe Dr. Adrian. She didn't *feel* safe here. Jordan had warned her that he used lies to make himself appear trustworthy and good.

"You kidnapped us and you're holding us against our will," Grace said.

"Grace, I didn't intend to kidnap you and your family," Dr. Adrian said kindly. "But Jordan was in the way, and I'm positive he wouldn't have let you all come and stay with me if I'd invited you in the first place."

"Now that Jordan's . . . gone, will you release me and my family to go back home?"

Please say you'll let us go. I don't know how much more I can take being stuck here.

Dr. Adrian shook his head, pretending to look sad. "Unfortunately, I cannot let you and your family leave. Like I said, you'll be safe here, not out there in the chaotic world. You think it's chaotic now, but just wait till I start my plan. I wouldn't want you all to get hurt while I'm taking over the world."

Grace pretended to cry at the news that she and her family weren't going home. Dr. Adrian handed her a tissue.

He's falling for the act.

Dr. Adrian sat there for a moment, letting Grace wipe her eyes. Then he said kindly, "At least you're still alive and well. That's all that matters."

"Yes, I suppose so," Grace said weakly.

I can't believe that he believes my fake charade. I better keep it up for now.

"I want you to learn to trust me, Grace," Dr. Adrian said, growing businesslike again. "All the things your brother told you about me are lies."

"I'll learn to trust you, but it'll take some time," Grace said, leaning back in her chair.

"Of course, Grace. I understand that. If there's anything you want to talk to me about, you can," Dr. Adrian said kindly, smiling a little bit.

I can see right through your façade, Dr. Adrian.

"But right now, there's some information I need to tell you," Dr. Adrian said.

■■■■■■■■■■■■■■■■■■

Jordan woke up to the smell of bacon.

Looks like someone's up.

He threw on a shirt and jeans, then grabbed his things from his desk and slung his bag over his shoulder. As he went down the stairs, he could hear several people speaking in the kitchen.

How come they didn't send someone to wake me up?

Entering the kitchen, Jordan found the entire group eating breakfast. Oliver was at the stove cooking something.

"Thanks for the wakeup call, everyone," Jordan said, picking up a plate and putting a waffle and some bacon on it.

Lucas made a choking sound.

"Lucas, did you just inhale your bacon again?" Jace asked, trying not to smile.

"Yeah," Lucas said hoarsely before taking a sip of juice.

"We figured we'd let you sleep in," Wyatt said to Jordan.

"Gee, thanks," Jordan said sarcastically, sitting down between Lucas and Wyatt.

"How are the waffles, Jordan?" Oliver asked, sitting down at the kitchen table.

"Great, thanks," Jordan said with his mouth full.

Oliver smiled. "Glad you like them. I have a feeling we won't be eating much home-cooked food after today."

Nodding, Jordan ate another bite of waffle and then chased it down with a swig of orange juice.

"How long's the drive to Montana?" Theodore asked.

Jordan looked up from his plate. "Ten hours and twenty-one minutes, not including breaks and gas."

"Seriously, that long?" Nate asked, eyes wide.

Jordan nodded as he hurried to finish his food.

"When do you think we should leave?" Jace asked.

"In the next hour or two," Jordan said, standing. "I'll check how much gas Levi's spare car has."

This is it. Once we leave Boise, there's no going back.

With nine of them, they had to take two cars, Oliver's as well as Levi's. After putting their luggage in the trunks, everyone piled in.

"Are we all ready to go?" Jace asked from the front passenger seat of Levi's car.

"Yes," came a small chorus of replies.

Jordan started the car. "If anybody wants to back out of the mission, speak now or forever hold your peace."

The silence grew, soon becoming uncomfortably quiet.

As Jordan headed toward the interstate, Jace turned on the radio and found some music.

About an hour into the drive, Jace pointed out that Jordan's knuckles were white from holding the steering wheel so tight.

"I didn't even notice I was doing that," Jordan replied sheepishly as he carefully relaxed his grip.

"Is everything okay?" Jace whispered, leaning towards Jordan.

"Yeah, I think I'm fine," Jordan whispered back as he continued to watch the road.

Am I really all right? Or have I just said that for so long that I think I'm fine, when I'm not?

"Jordan, it's going to be okay," Jace said in a low voice. "We're going to get your family back. We all promised that on our lives. We may stare death in the face just to save them, but we're going to do it for their sake."

Jordan glanced at Jace and knew he was right, but something was still nagging at him. "It's just—since my parents died, I set my whole life on looking for Grace. I didn't think she would get kidnapped like this. I'm the one who's supposed to get kidnapped. It'd be much easier breaking myself out than trying to save Grace and the others from the outside."

Glancing in the rearview mirror, Jordan saw that everyone was watching him and Jace. "Should we be wondering what you two are talking about?" Nate half-joked from the very back.

"No, don't worry about it," Jace said, turning around to face everyone. "It's nothing that concerns the rest of you."

In the rearview mirror, Jordan saw that the guys were giving each other side glances.

A few minutes later, Jace whispered to Jordan, "Do you really think it'll be *that* hard to save your family?"

"It depends on how strong Dr. Adrian's security is in that building right now," Jordan whispered back, getting off at an exit.

"Why are we getting off here?" Nate asked from the back, pulling out an earbud and looking out the window. "I thought we still have a long time before we get to Montana."

"To get gas and let everyone stretch," Jordan said, pulling into a gas station.

While Jordan and Oliver pumped gas, the other guys either headed over to use the restroom or just walked around the parking lot. When his tank was full, Jordan went inside and bought himself two bottles of water, an energy drink, a candy bar, and a bag of chips.

Sometime later, as it was growing dark, Jordan pulled over so Jace could take a turn driving.

"Do you think Dr. Adrian has done anything bad to your family?" Jace asked once they were underway again. Everyone in back seemed to be asleep, so he used a normal voice.

"No, I don't think so," said Jordan. "Dr. Adrian believes I'm dead, so I'm sure he's celebrating."

After a while, Jordan's head began to bob.

"You can fall asleep if you want," said Jace. "You don't have to stay awake."

Nodding, Jordan adjusted his position and quickly fell asleep.

Sometime later, he jolted awake. The car wasn't moving,

and Jace was asleep. He had pulled the car into an empty parking lot next to a park. Oliver's car was parked next to Levi's car.

I need some fresh air. I can't stand being in the car. I just need to be by myself and get my thoughts together.

Jordan quietly unlocked his car door and got out. In the dark, he noticed someone walking towards him from the other side of the parking lot. Jordan's first instinct was to fight. But as moments passed, he realized it was Oliver.

"Couldn't sleep?" Oliver asked, sitting down on a curb.

"Not anymore, I guess," Jordan said, sitting down next to Oliver.

"Leading a group can put you under a lot of stress," Oliver admitted, looking towards the park.

"Yeah," Jordan said, nodding. "How long have you been up?"

"Well, it's about one in the morning. I think I've been up since, like, twelve. I didn't check my phone. I just wanted to get out of the car. The breeze feels nice right about now."

Soon, Jordan was lost in his thoughts again. He hardly noticed when Oliver slapped him on the back and got up to go back in the car.

Sometime later, Henry came over and shook Jordan, who was still sitting on the curb, dozing off and on.

"How long have you been out here, Jordan?" Henry questioned, sitting down.

"Since about one," Jordan said, rubbing his eyes. "What time is it now?"

"Almost seven," Henry said. "Is all the stress of leading the group getting to you?"

"Yeah, very much so," Jordan quietly said, trying to stay

awake.

"Jordan, you need to get some real sleep. I'll tell Jace you can't drive."

"No, it's fine—I'll tell him myself." Jordan got up from the curb.

As Jace drove back to the freeway, Jordan fell asleep again.

Sometime later, Jace tapped Jordan on the shoulder. It was full daylight outside, maybe even afternoon. Sitting up straight, Jordan stretched his arms and rubbed his eyes.

"We've been in Montana for a while," said Jace. "I thought I better wake you up so you can tell us the plan."

Pulling out his phone, Jordan opened a map app. For the next couple hours, he guided Jace where to drive. After they left the freeway, the roads got progressively smaller and were surrounded by more trees.

"Pull over in that rest area," Jordan finally said. "We'll have to ditch the cars and walk the rest of the way to the building. I'll tell the group the plan on the hike there."

Jace nodded and pulled over, causing everyone to look around bewildered.

"Why are we stopping here?" Nate asked, looking out the window.

"We have to hike the rest of the way through the trees, otherwise Dr. Adrian's security will catch us," Jordan explained, getting out of the car.

"Are you still bringing all your tech with you?" Wyatt asked, climbing out of the car.

"Yeah, I still have to track where Grace is," Jordan said, putting his laptop into his backpack. "If I know Dr. Adrian, he'll have her close to him. Shall we get started?"

A few hours later, Jordan signaled the group to stop. Sitting on a fallen tree trunk, he pulled out his computer and looked at it for a few moments. As Jace watched Jordan, he wondered what the next phase of the plan would be.

"All right," Jordan finally said. "So, for the rest of the way, there are guard posts. The trees are going to thin out, so we'll have to wait till night before we sneak into the building. Once we're there, I'll tell you how we're going to get in."

Jace and the others nodded numbly, not saying anything. *I doubt we'll get any sleep tonight,* Jace thought to himself.

As if hearing Jace's thought, Jordan said, "Try to get some sleep, because you all look dead. I'll be lookout and secure the perimeter."

"Sounds like a great idea," Oliver muttered. Everyone lay on the ground or sat with their back against a tree.

Using his backpack as a pillow, Jace quickly fell asleep. Sometime later, Jordan shook him awake.

"What?" Jace asked groggily, rubbing the sleep from his eyes.

"It's dusk now. If you need to eat something or do anything else, now's the time," Jordan said.

"How long was I out?" Jace asked as he stretched.

"I don't know," Jordan admitted. "I just came back from securing the perimeter."

"Where's everyone else?" Jace asked, suddenly realizing the rest of the group was gone.

"They're safe," Jordan said simply, a dark smile on his face. "Let me show you where they are."

Jordan is acting really weird. He's never smiled like that.

As Jace followed Jordan through the trees, several guards sprang out and surrounded them. Jace let out a cry, wondering how Jordan was going to get them out of this.

"Put your hands in the air!" one guard shouted, pointing a gun at Jace.

Jace did what he was told. A guard then cuffed his hands, nodding at Jordan.

"Take him away," Jordan said to the guards.

"Yes, sir, Dr. Adrian!" the guards said in unison.

Jace felt shocked. *Why does he look like Jordan?*

▪▪▪▪▪▪▪▪▪▪▪▪▪▪▪▪▪▪

Dr. Adrian smiled darkly, knowing that Jordan's friends were caught.

"I still can't believe Jordan didn't die," he muttered to himself. "I thought all that stabbing would surely kill him."

Appearing in the doorway, Grant stood at attention. "Sir, you requested me to come to your office?"

"Yes, Grant, come in," Dr. Adrian said, gesturing to one of the chairs. "Have any of Jordan's friends cracked yet and told us any useful information?"

"Nope," Grant said, shaking his head. "They're all tight as clams. They won't tell us anything."

"Has anybody found Jordan yet?" Dr. Adrian asked, voice

going cold.

"No, sir," Grant said. "He's disappeared and eluded our trackers once again."

"What do you mean?" Dr. Adrian growled. "I thought he was near enough that you could track him. Especially since he still has at least one tracker in him! When he was in Boise, we could track him then. How come we can't track him now?"

Grant flinched as Dr. Adrian yelled. When Dr. Adrian was done, Grant quietly said, "I—I don't know, Dr. Adrian. The guards in charge of the trackers are doing everything they can to track Jordan down and bring him back here."

"Well, they're not doing a good job then!" Dr. Adrian shouted.

Grant flinched again, but then his face grew resolved. "Dr. Adrian, why are you worried about a boy, especially since he *could* be dead? What if his friends came here on their own to avenge their leader's death?"

"I know Jordan is alive," Dr. Adrian said. "I controlled his mind long enough to get his group captured. But as the last of his friends was being dragged away, Jordan gathered enough strength and willpower to shield his mind from me."

Folding his arms, Grant remained silent.

With effort, Dr. Adrian softened his expression. In a kind voice, he asked, "Could you please bring in Grace?"

"Yes, sir," Grant said, rising from the chair.

Dr. Adrian waited patiently.

A few dozen yards from Dr. Adrian's building, Jordan moved stealthily among the trees, feeling like a failure.

I can't believe it took me so long to block Dr. Adrian from my mind. I just got my entire group caught. Now I have to figure out how to save my family and *my friends.*

Hiding behind a tree, Jordan looked closely at the building. Helmeted guards stood all along the building's perimeter, and on top, Jordan could see several manned watch posts. He felt a wave of frustration go through him.

As Jordan thought about possible next steps, his confidence grew but he felt some misgivings. *I'm going to have to use the pinpoint power and specifically target all the guards outside the building. Then I can search their bodies for the keys to get inside. Once I'm inside, the guards will be on high alert. But hopefully, I'll have a chance to figure out the next step of the plan.*

Closing his eyes, Jordan pictured all the guards around and atop the building and then unleashed his power onto his enemies.

As the moments passed, Jordan fell to his knees. His entire body was shaking, but he still pushed his power. In the corners of his eyes, fuzzy darkness was starting to take away his vision. He knew he was losing consciousness, but he continued to use his power.

After a few minutes, Jordan stopped his power and listened intently for any signs that the guards were still up. His excellent hearing told him that the guards were all unconscious. It was silent all around him, except for his own heavy breathing. No alarms had sounded during his attack.

Well, so far the plan has gone well. Let's see if the rest works out.

Leaving the trees, Jordan made his way down to search the nearest guard's body. In the guard's pocket, he found two keys and a swipe card. He removed the guard's uniform and his own shirt and pants, then pulled on the uniform, including the helmet. Oddly enough, the uniform fit him very well.

Grabbing his backpack, Jordan moved forward. Using the keys, he was able to open the building's outer gate and door. He strode into the building, trying to act as confident as possible. The helmet's mask covered his entire face, so he wasn't worried about giving away his cover.

I need to find the elevator that'll take me to the cells. That's where I'll hopefully find my friends and family.

Spotting an elevator, Jordan swiped the card to gain entry. After looking around the elevator nervously, he pushed the button with the letter C on it, which he vaguely remembered might stand for *cellblock.*

When the elevator doors opened, he walked out into what was indeed a cellblock. The hallway lights were turned down. *This side of the building was always a lot darker than the rest of the building.*

Jordan walked confidently down the hallway towards the guards' video surveillance room. He swiped his card and walked right in.

"What are you doing here?" a guard said, standing up. "There isn't a new shift till tonight."

"I know, but Dr. Adrian sent me to get you," Jordan said coolly, playing the part of a guard on duty. "He wants to speak with you."

The guard looked mildly surprised.

Jordan used his pinpoint power, and the guard collapsed almost immediately. He slid out his computer and looked up the tracker to see where Grace was. To his disappointment, she was with Dr. Adrian in his office.

I'll have to get her later. For now, let's see where my friends and the rest of my family are.

Jordan moved his attention to the video consoles, which showed various empty and occupied cells.

Come on. Where are you guys?

Before long, he found Jace lying alone in a cell. His heart leapt for joy as he looked at his best friend. Finding paper and pencil, he wrote down Jace's cell number. Then he scrolled through more video cameras until he found Colton and Devon, who were in the same cell. *Well, that made searching for those two easier.*

After he'd found everyone and noted their cell numbers, Jordan made his way to Jace's cell. He unlocked Jace's cell and walked in. Jace whipped around and was about to lunge at Jordan, but Jordan quickly pulled off his helmet.

"Jordan! What are you doing here?" Jace asked, looking confused. "I thought Dr. Adrian captured you."

"Dr. Adrian was controlling my mind, but he couldn't get me," Jordan said. "I'm here to get you out."

"Hooray," Jace said. As the two of them walked out into the hallway, he asked, "Have you found where everyone is?"

"Everyone but Grace, I'm afraid," Jordan said. "Dr. Adrian has her up in his office. Let's go get Lucas—he's next on my list."

Just then, a high-pitched alarm went off.

Jordan quickly put the helmet back on so he wouldn't blow his cover. "The guard at the control center must have woken up," he said, frantically looking around for a hiding place. "Or maybe another guard noticed you were gone."

"Uh, Jordan, we have company," Jace said.

Turning, Jordan saw two guards walking down the hallway towards them. The ear-piercing alarm had kept him from hearing them.

"What are you doing with that prisoner?" one of the guards asked, putting his hand on his gun.

"Dr. Adrian told me to bring him up for questioning," Jordan said, hoping the guard would take the lie.

"Dr. Adrian is still talking to that girl," the guard responded.

"And apparently Thurgood's inside the building. The guard at the control center said he used a power against him."

"Well, I have my orders," Jordan said. "I wouldn't want to go against the boss. Are we sure Thurgood's inside the building, or is he pulling some kind of mental stunt?"

All right, this charade has gone on long enough.

Before the guard could respond, Jordan used his pinpoint power and made them both fall to the ground unconscious.

"I was wondering when you'd do that," Jace said.

"Quick, help me drag them," Jordan said, pointing to a nearby empty cell.

After they'd moved the guards, Jace took the equipment and uniform from one. He pulled on the uniform he thought would fit best, but it was quite loose.

"What do we do now?" Jace asked as Jordan locked the cell door behind them.

"I'm not sure. Maybe try to blend in with the other guards and pretend to look for me. And stay as far away from Dr. Adrian and Grant as possible. We really don't want to mess with them."

Jordan headed down a hallway, and Jace walked alongside him, a hand on his gun holster.

They ran into a group of three guards.

We are wasting so much time just walking around the freaking building. When will they turn off that awful alarm and give up searching for me?

"What are you boys doing?" the head guard questioned, blocking their way.

"We're just doing our jobs, sir," Jace responded.

"Show me your IDs," the guard ordered, stepping closer to Jordan and Jace.

"Oh, sure," Jordan said, patting his pockets. Jace started doing the same.

The guard stood there impatiently. "Will you two hurry up? I need to make sure this level is secure from Thurgood."

"Yeah, yeah, just give me a second," Jordan muttered.

Using his pinpoint power, he dropped the guards to the ground.

"This is getting annoying," Jordan said, turning to Jace. "Not just the alarm, but having to drop guards left and right. We need to go back to the control center and see if we can turn off the alarm."

Dodging and backtracking away from several more patrolling guards, they finally reached the control room. After looking at the controls for what seemed like an eternity, they managed to turn off the alarm. Then they used the intercom to announce that it was a false alarm and Thurgood was not in the building.

The guards grumbled and swore, but returned to their positions.

"We need to quickly grab the others, get Grace, and get out of here," Jordan said.

After the random false alarm, Dr. Adrian reluctantly allowed Grace to go back to her room with a guard stationed outside her door, while he dealt with whoever had pulled the alarm and caused panic in the building.

Grace walked around her room, looking at nothing in particular. She was still deciding whether to trust Dr. Adrian. Jordan had warned her countless times that Dr. Adrian would lie and do everything in his power to get someone to trust him.

When she heard her door being unlocked, she snapped out of her thoughts. A helmeted guard walked in.

"What do you want?" Grace asked bitterly.

"Grace, it's me," the guard said.

This guard sounds awfully familiar . . .

"Jordan?" Grace asked, embracing her brother.

Jordan hugged her tightly with one arm, using his other hand to take off his helmet.

"I can't believe you're here," Grace said, pulling back from her brother.

"Well, I certainly wasn't going to let Dr. Adrian brainwash you and turn you into a mutant like me," Jordan said.

Grace smiled and nodded, thinking of Jordan's powers.

"Let's get out of this place," Jordan said, shuddering. "I've spent enough time here today to last me a lifetime."

Nodding again, Grace followed Jordan out of her room.

In the hallway, Jordan's family held a brief, happy reunion, with lots of hugging from friends. Now all thirteen of Jordan's people were free.

"Let's get out of here," Jordan said tensely.

They didn't make it far before the alarm started going off again.

"I knew this would happen," Jordan muttered. "One of the

guards I knocked unconscious must have woken up."

A second later, the alarm stopped.

Everyone looked around tensely, wondering what to do.

Just then, a voice came over the intercom. "Jordan—what a lovely surprise," Dr. Adrian said. "You could've called me, and we would've arranged a meeting."

"Yeah, right," Jordan said, looking up at the intercom box. "Last time we met, you killed me and then kidnapped my family."

His family looked over at him quizzically, but he shook his head and mouthed, "Not now."

Nodding, his family turned their attention back to the intercom.

"Well, when I killed you, I thought you'd stay out of my way so I could take over the world with little or no resistance," Dr. Adrian retorted. "But I was wrong. Just when I thought my plan was going well, you decided to show up."

Jordan was silent, his jaw clenched shut.

"I did miss the fight you always gave when you were here," Dr. Adrian continued. "Your sister does exactly what I want with little or no fighting. I've missed that struggle. No offense, Grace."

"Of course you missed our fights and arguments," Jordan said. "You miss torturing me because it gave you an adrenaline rush. You miss having me kill people for you and nobody suspecting it was you, because you let the reporters drag my name through the mud. You miss all the bragging rights you got when I was your trained little lap dog and my missions went according to plan. You miss all the power you had because I was your only successful creation."

"Well, now I'm just hurt, Jordan," Dr. Adrian said defensively. "You don't talk to your dad like that."

Jordan shook his head in disgust. *Is he really calling himself my dad? You've got to be kidding me. Dr. Adrian's gotten even crazier since I've last encountered him.*

"You're certainly not my dad, Dr. Adrian!" Jordan shouted at the intercom. "I've never thought of you as that. And I never will!"

"You need to learn some manners, Jordan," Dr. Adrian said, his voice growing hard. "You did think of me as your dad at one point. You can't deny that. You're just afraid to admit it."

"You're really getting on my nerves, Dr. Adrian. Did you know that?"

Dr. Adrian was silent for a moment, clearly a bit surprised at Jordan's outburst. He finally said, "Likewise, Jordan. And yet, you still manage to come back again and again, almost as if you really do like this little game."

Jordan laughed. "You're the one who started the game. If your priorities weren't all screwed up and you weren't focusing on the wrong things, I might not have had to fight back. You claim you're going to save the world by taking it over. You claim you've never killed anyone, and yet you took my life. Stop lying, Dr. Adrian."

"Oh, really, Jordan?" Dr. Adrian said, his voice sounding agitated. "You really want to start causing more drama? You chose this life on the run. You chose to fight against me. I tried to help you have a better life, but you just wouldn't accept my help."

Tears glistened in Jordan's eyes. "I chose to be free! Free from you. Free to choose the life I want for myself, not the one you planned. You're so blinded by greed and power, Dr. Adrian, that you can't see the harm your plan will cause. Nobody else is going to stand up to you, so why not me?"

Dr. Adrian fell silent.

Standing together in the hallway, Jordan's friends and family stared at him in bewilderment.

Jordan shook his head and mouthed, "I'll explain later," his eyes pleading.

"I have guards surrounding the hallway," Dr. Adrian said a few moments later. "There is no escape. Surrender now, and I'll let your family and friends have a pleasant time here with me."

"Do whatever you like to me, Dr. Adrian, but you're not doing anything to my family or my friends," Jordan shot back.

"Now that's what I like about you, Jordan. You're always trying to sacrifice yourself to protect others. I wonder if you ever get tired of it."

Jordan was silent as several moments seemed to pass slowly. Finally, he said, "I've never gotten tired of being a hero. I'm willing to do things that nobody else wants to do. That includes stopping you from taking over the world."

Dr. Adrian fell silent again.

Jordan said, "I see you've lost your words, Dr. Adrian. I'll let you gather your thoughts, and you can tell me next time you see me."

"I haven't lost my words, Jordan," Dr. Adrian retorted. "I'm just saving them for when I do have to see you in person, which will be very soon."

Jordan looked around, and sure enough, guards were blocking their exit on both ends of the hallway.

Why did I not hear them coming? My hearing would've picked up people moving towards us.

"You pull the same stunts every time," Jordan said to the

intercom. "It's kind of getting old. Even my friends and family are bored out of their minds." He winked at his people, hoping they'd get the hint and play along with it.

"What do you mean, the same stunts every time?" Dr. Adrian said, growing angry. "I've always changed them up."

"You may think you have, but they're always the same every time I run into you," Jordan said nonchalantly. He smiled at his friends and family, who were looking worriedly at him.

Wyatt mouthed back, "You trying to get us killed?"

Jordan shook his head and then pointed to his own forehead, indicating that he was going to use his pinpoint power on the guards.

His friends and family looked at him like he was crazy. They knew he'd never used his pinpoint power at full blast with people nearby who he didn't want to hurt.

"Trust me," Jordan mouthed to everyone in the hallway.

Here I go with my crazy plan that I made up in fifteen seconds. Let's see if it works.

Jordan willed himself to think about the guards, how much anger they'd caused him by taking his friends and family from him. As he concentrated his willpower, he called out, "If you want us so badly, Dr. Adrian, then come get us."

"Guards, don't let them escape!" Dr. Adrian nearly shouted.

The guards moved towards Jordan and his group.

Stretching out his arms, Jordan stopped the guards in their tracks. As they collapsed to the ground, several of them gasped audibly. Jordan increased his powers until many of the guards were shaking and groaning in pain.

When Jordan fell to his knees, Lucas and Nate rushed over and held him steady. Groaning, he lost his concentration for a moment, but then he regained enough strength to continue pushing his power onto the guards. He wondered what Dr. Adrian was thinking as he watched through the security camera.

Before long, the guards were visibly wounded by Jordan's power, and most of them were dead. Jordan's friends and family were silent as they watched him with both wonder and shock.

Finally, Jordan put his arms down and remained kneeling on the ground, with Lucas and Nate still supporting him. Fear gripped him as he realized that Dr. Adrian had just seen him use a power. He was going to be an even bigger target now that Dr. Adrian knew Jordan could use his powers.

After a few moments, Jordan lurched forward, feeling like he was going to pass out. Luckily, Lucas and Nate hadn't loosened their hold on him. This was the worst he'd ever felt after using the pinpoint power.

"Jordan, are you okay?" Nate asked, leaning closer to Jordan.

Jordan shook his head, feeling like he would throw up if he opened his mouth. It felt like a bunch of needles were pressing into his body. Hot tears fell from his eyes as he just knelt there looking at the ground, not saying a word. There was only so much pain he could take.

Some minutes later, the pain finally started to diminish. Looking down the hallway, Jordan noticed one of the guards lying curled up in a ball, whimpering softly to himself.

"Help me up," he said to Lucas and Nate. Once he was standing, Jordan grabbed a throwing knife from his belt and carefully aimed it at the video camera. When the knife hit the camera, it broke the glass lens. Jordan watched until the camera's red light died. He didn't want Dr. Adrian to see what he was going to do next.

Still supported by Lucas and Nate, Jordan slowly walked to

the whimpering guard and gently pressed his hand on the guard's back. The guard's body immediately relaxed.

Quietly the guard asked, "Are you healing me?"

Jordan nodded.

The guard sighed with relief as Jordan worked another one of his powers. After a couple minutes, the guard was able to sit up without crying out in pain. Jordan helped him pull off his helmet. To his surprise, he recognized the guard.

"Thank you so, so much," said the guard, looking directly into Jordan's eyes.

Nodding and smiling, Jordan remembered the man's name was Ben. "You helped me get out last time I was in here. You showed me the secret one-way passageway and distracted the other guards. You nearly died with me."

"Jordan, I can't believe it's you," said Ben, tears welling up in his eyes. "I remember everything. Dr. Adrian tortured me for helping you. But now you've healed me inside and out."

Jordan kept smiling, overcome by his emotions. By now, his friends and family had gathered around with amazed looks on their faces.

"So, what're you going to do next?" Ben asked, raising his eyebrows. "Dr. Adrian isn't going to stop hunting you down."

"Let's get out of here," Jordan said.

"After you get home, can I look you up?" Ben asked. "I've been wanting to quit this job and start over somewhere else with my family."

Jordan remembered than Ben and his wife had two kids who would now be in their teens. "Sure," he said. He pulled the list of cells from his pocket, wrote his Boise address on back, and handed the paper to Ben.

Ben smiled, his eyes shining with hope for a change in his

life. After expressing his thanks again, he headed down the hallway around the bodies of the other guards, walking like a man in full health.

"I think it's time to go home," Jordan said, turning back to his friends and family. "Don't want to overstay our welcome."

They nodded numbly, still shocked about the turn of events.

As they walked out the same way Jordan had come in, Wyatt broke the silence. "I didn't know you had healing powers."

Jordan smiled. "I didn't know either. My intuition told me to touch Ben."

Nate broke in. "Does Dr. Adrian know about your healing and pinpoint powers?"

Jordan nodded. "He knew I had powers, but his tests couldn't tell him which ones. I'm still learning about them myself. The stronger my emotions are, the stronger my powers are. I was so angry at Dr. Adrian that my pinpoint power physically wounded the guards, which I haven't seen before. And the aftereffect on me was worse as well, as you saw."

"That was the maddest I've seen you in a long time, and that's saying something," Braxton said, shaking his head in wonder.

I already knew my powers were dangerous, but if I can't keep my emotions in check, I could possibly hurt or kill millions.

"Why do you have powers, while other people don't?" Colton asked as the large group hiked through the trees.

"Well," Jordan said, thinking for a moment. "I was a test subject for one of Dr. Adrian's plans to make people into mutants with powers. I was the only person who survived the test. And nobody knows why."

CHAPTER 32

Jordan finally drove Levi's car into the garage at about two in the morning. After the others woke up and groggily went to their bedrooms, Jordan stayed in the car for a few minutes, thinking.

I know I'll have to leave again, so I don't put my family in even more danger. They don't know how much danger they're already in, even though they said they'd go with me for the rest of my mission.

Jordan thought back to what Grace had said when he'd told her one of his concerns: "We're not leaving you, Jordan. You're the one who put your life in danger, just to rescue us all. I might as well stay by you—that's how I'll repay you."

Well, the drive home from Montana was a lot calmer than going. All my friends and family got away without a scratch on them.

Jordan finally got out of the car and headed into the house to go to bed and start another day.

■■■■■■■■■■■■■■■■■■

As the weeks passed after the rescue mission, Jordan and his friends and family were careful not to talk about what had happened except among themselves. They all felt that the rescue should be kept private. They saw news reports about the incident, but they all knew the reports were false. They knew what *really* happened.

Sitting on the couch one afternoon doing science homework, Jordan let his mind wander again to the rescue mission and Dr. Adrian. He recalled the adrenaline rush he'd felt while saving his friends and family. He knew that he needed to follow the headmaster's orders and go end Dr. Adrian and save the world from utter destruction.

I better get to the gym before my dad comes home.

Setting his computer aside, Jordan got up from the couch and walked to the garage, car keys in hand. As he approached, he heard the garage door rattling open. To his surprise, his dad was pulling into the double garage's open space.

"So, where you running off to, Jordan?" Levi asked casually as he got out of his car.

Jordan hesitated for a moment. "To the gym."

His dad looked at him with a serious expression. "All right. Just be back before dinner."

Jordan smiled. "Will do, Dad."

Jordan got into Levi's spare car, backed out of the garage, and drove away.

■■■■■■■■■■■■■■■■■■■■

Levi felt a little sad as he watched Jordan leave.

I haven't seen much of Jordan lately. He's usually at the gym or with his friends. I wonder if they're making plans to leave again.

Levi Greenfield felt that he had strong bonds with all three of his adopted teens. But Jordan had seemed a little distant and reserved since they'd all gotten back from Montana.

Levi sighed, going inside the house.

"How was your day, guys?" Levi asked, sitting down at the kitchen table near Grace and Braxton.

"Mine was pretty good," Braxton responded simply.

"My day was good," Grace said, looking up from her homework. "How was your day, Dad?"

"Well, it's been good. Do you know why Jordan's been so . . . distant lately?" Levi asked. He hoped that maybe Grace or Braxton had gotten some information out of him.

Grace replied, "He hasn't said anything to me."

Braxton shrugged. "Yeah, he's been more distant than usual. I think that rescue mission has got him thinking about continuing the mission the headmaster gave him."

"That's what I thought," Levi said, slowly nodding. "Has Henry said anything about another mission?"

Grace thought for a moment. "Actually, he has. Let me pull up our texts." Grabbing her phone, she scrolled in silence and then handed the phone to Levi. "Here they are. I know they're still finalizing some plans, but Henry told me the gist of the mission."

Levi read through the texts. "Sounds like the plan to drive to California and go to the Academy is still happening. And probably soon, from the sound of the texts. Just like what Jordan wanted to do before we were kidnapped."

"At least he's still going through with the original plan," Grace said.

Levi nodded, staring off into space, too lost in his thoughts to say anything.

When Jordan got home from the gym, Levi handed him a large, thick manila envelope. "This came in today's mail. It looks important."

Jordan flipped over the envelope to check the return address. When he saw the name, the corners of his mouth twitched into a smile. "It's from the headmaster."

"Well, open it," Levi said.

"I want the rest of the guys here when I open it," Jordan said. "I'll text them now."

An hour later, Jace and Wyatt were the last to arrive.

"What took you guys so long?" Nate asked, lightly punching Wyatt on the arm.

"You try living on the other side of town, and then tell me how it goes when you try to get here as fast as possible," Jace shot back.

Nate stepped away from Jace, putting up his hands in surrender.

"Anyway," Jordan said, giving Jace a side glance. "How about we open the envelope and see what's inside?"

Standing in the living room, Jordan looked around at his friends and family, all together again for the first time since

Montana. Grace, Braxton, and Levi sat together on the large sofa. His school friends—Henry, James, and Theodore—sat cross-legged on the floor. His Academy roommates, Jace and Wyatt, sat in the love seat. And his three Academy friends—Oliver, Nate, and Lucas—stood together behind the sofa.

"Open it!" Wyatt nearly shouted.

Let's see what the headmaster has to say. Hopefully it's some good news.

After tearing open the envelope, Jordan pulled out a stack of papers. On top was a letter, which he read aloud:

Dear Jordan,

We've been compromised and need your help. Someone in the Academy tipped Dr. Adrian that we're planning an attack against him. I'm writing to you personally because I know you'd like some revenge on Dr. Adrian for all the things he's done to you.

In this envelope are the plans for our attacks. Find everyone from the Academy you're still in contact with, and tell them these plans.

Remember when I told you that you had lots of potential to do great and dangerous things? Well, now I need you more than ever. I heard that you got Grace and your family out of one of Dr. Adrian's buildings. I also heard that you used two of your powers. I applaud you for both of those accomplishments.

Now here's a real mission for you, something you've been training for your whole life. I hope you remember what I've been teaching you. Use your powers for good, not just to hurt people, like what you did to save your friends and family.

The

Headmaster

Jordan looked up at his friends and family. They were all silent, waiting to see what plans the headmaster was talking about.

How does the headmaster know I have powers?

"Let's spread these out on the kitchen table," Jordan said. They moved to the kitchen, and Jordan arranged the pages of the plan so everyone could see them.

"Jordan, how do you understand these?" asked Oliver. "There's too much small writing all over the place. I'd have to get a magnifying glass." Several others voiced their agreement with Oliver.

"I guess I'm just used to it," Jordan responded, looking down at the first page. "For starters, the headmaster wants us all at the Academy for training, including my family."

Jordan looked at Levi, who raised his eyebrows.

"So, this doesn't really change our California plan," Henry said.

"Not at all—it just gives us more reason to leave ASAP," said Jordan. "I'm hoping to leave tomorrow, if everyone agrees. When we get to the Academy, the first thing I'll do is have the headmaster scan me so we can take out the tracker."

Jordan looked around at everyone, feeling anxious. *Hopefully, these plans will work. I must keep in mind that we're doing this for the headmaster, for the Academy, and for the world.*

■■■■■■■■■■■■■■■■■

Dr. Adrian looked down at the papers on his desk, anger welling up inside him. According to one report, one of his guards had left during the chaos of Jordan and his family and friends escaping.

"I should've killed Jordan again when I had the chance," Dr. Adrian said, bitter hatred filling his voice. He thought back to that day when he'd ended Jordan's life in his dad's office. *How is he still alive?*

Glancing at one of his video monitors, he noticed some scientists talking in a small group, looking excited about something. *I'm sure I'll get a report later today about whatever they found so exciting.*

Dr. Adrian turned his attention back to the reports. *I lost a lot of great guards because of Jordan's insistence on misusing his powers. Once again, I must find more guards to hire. He needs to be stopped at all costs. At first, he was such a good boy. He would do everything I asked of him. But ever since he got those powers, he thinks he's entitled to everything. I miss the Jordan I had before he got his crazy fantasies about being a hero and saving the world.*

That evening, as Dr. Adrian was driving home, he started having someone else's thoughts. Instantly he recognized the thoughts as coming from Jordan.

You're the one who ruined my life, Dr. Adrian. Are you proud of that? That's not what you created your company to do. You were supposed to help people and make the world safer. But instead, in your own greed, you decided to see if you could turn people into mutants. Now you just want to hurt people and make them fear you.

I trusted you. At first, we had a strong relationship. You were like the dad I never had. But when you became greedy for power and money, I knew I couldn't keep quiet. I didn't want to become corrupt and hungry for power and money like you. I really don't want to fight you, Dr. Adrian, but I'm willing to die for what I believe in.

By the time Jordan's thoughts ended, Dr. Adrian felt shaken to the core. He started rethinking what he was doing. He wasn't going to forget those extremely powerful words any time soon.

CHAPTER 33

Jordan lay in bed, consumed in his thoughts. He knew his message had successfully entered Dr. Adrian's head, because he could feel Dr. Adrian's emotions changing even as he transmitted his thoughts.

I hate that connection we have. Now I can see and hear his thoughts, and in return he can see and hear mine.

Jordan looked over at his alarm clock. It was four in the morning. *I can never sleep anymore. That's what it's come to. I'm constantly up all night long.*

He turned over onto his left side, still wide awake. *I can't believe we're going to California. I finally get to go back to the Academy after so many years since my mission began.*

Jordan climbed out of bed, knowing he wasn't going to fall asleep. He walked over to his desk, sat down, and turned on the lamp, blinking several times until his eyes adjusted to the light.

Staring off into space, he took stock of his emotions. He could feel some anxiety, but not as much as he would have felt earlier in his life.

Jordan's eyes fell upon his guitar, standing in the corner. *Most of the songs I wrote before I started my mission were basically about coping with my anxiety. I was so worried about school and my mission. And now look at me. I'm not afraid of things that I used to be afraid of.*

I used to be afraid to die. I already died once but then came back to life, proving my powers. I was afraid of losing my friends, and I lost contact with them for a long time, but then reconnected with them. I was afraid of how people might hurt me and use me like Dr. Adrian did, but the people I've now surrounded myself with haven't hurt me or used me for their own personal gain.

Jordan felt a sense of triumph for all the fears he'd conquered so far in his life.

He got up, walked over to the mirror, and studied himself. Tracing the scars on his arms, he felt self-conscious about them for a few moments.

I wonder what kind of person I'd be now if I'd never accepted the invitation to go to the Academy and undertake this important mission.

Jordan's mind wandered to Emma, the girl he'd liked at the Academy all those years ago. *I wonder if she's still in love with me at all. I wouldn't be surprised if she secretly dumped me for a guy who wasn't as wild and crazy as I am.*

Jordan pushed that thought out of his mind—he knew he couldn't worry right now about anything but California. He needed to put all his focus on the tasks that lay ahead.

Jordan breathed deeply, held his breath for a few moments, then exhaled. This exercise helped him cope with stress. And right then, he was under a lot of stress.

Grace woke up at six that morning, confused for a moment about where she was. But when she looked around, she knew she was in her own bedroom at Levi's house.

I wonder if anybody else is up.

Grace made her bed and started getting ready. Today was the day she would go to California with her friends and family.

As she packed, someone knocked on her door.

"Come in," she called out.

Colton opened the door and walked in. "Hey, sis," he said, sitting down on Grace's bed. "Are you nervous about all this?"

Grace thought for a moment. "No, not really. I knew we'd have to leave sooner or later. It was just a matter of time before the headmaster contacted Jordan and told him to go to California with anybody who was willing. Why do you ask?"

Colton looked uncomfortable. "Because I'm afraid about the mission. I'm afraid that while we're saving the world, one of our family members or friends is going to die."

Over the few weeks that Colton, Devon, and Madison had been around, Grace had grown close with her potential new stepmother and stepbrothers. She was closest with Colton, while Jordan and Braxton were closest with Devon.

"Colton, as long as we're with Jordan, he'll make sure we're all safe. When we get to the Academy, lots of people will make sure we're safe. And once we leave the Academy, we'll be prepared to face Dr. Adrian and his army."

Colton nodded and smiled slightly. "Thank you, Grace. That actually helps a lot."

"Anytime, Colton," Grace said, returning Colton's smile.

She felt deep respect for Colton and looked up to him. In some ways, he reminded her of Elijah, her former foster brother who'd protected her. Like Elijah, Colton was kind, honest, trustworthy, great at keeping secrets, and responsible.

As she thought of Elijah, a twinge of sadness welled up inside her. Her old family had never tried to contact her, and so she'd never tried to contact them. If they'd wanted to see her, they would've found her contact information.

They never loved me. They were too self-absorbed. They just used me for their own personal gain and never actually took care of me. That's what most of my life was like until Levi found me and adopted me.

Colton got up from her bed, walked over to her, and hugged her for a moment. "Are you okay, Grace?" he whispered.

Grace looked up, tears in her eyes. "Yeah, I'm fine." She quickly brushed away the tears.

Nodding, Colton hugged her tighter for a moment, letting the silence of the house envelope them. Then he stepped back. "I better let you finish packing. I'll talk to you later."

At about nine, all of Jordan's friends and family were gathered in the living room, ready to go. Their stuff was loaded into both of Levi's cars.

"All right, let's decide who's going in which car," Jordan said.

The living room filled with voices as everyone figured out who was going with whom. When the room became quiet again, Jordan said, "Raise your hand if you're going with me."

Jace, Devon, James, Braxton, Oliver, and Nate raised their hands.

Jordan nodded. "All right, let's get out of here."

The room exploded with voices as everyone said goodbye for now to those riding in the other car.

This is really happening. After all this time, I finally get to go to back to the Academy and see the headmaster.

Once everyone was seated in the cars, Jordan backed out of the garage first, leading the way. For the first little while, the car was silent, everyone wearing a serious, subdued expression. Jordan wondered if they were all thinking the same thing: *Are we going to live through this battle and make it back home?*

Jordan was used to leaving places, but this time it felt different. He'd made so many friends and memories in Boise, and he didn't want to leave it all behind.

He looked over at Nate, sitting in the front passenger seat. "I'm surprised you haven't said something punny or cracked a joke yet, Nate."

Nate laughed. "Well, I do have a joke in mind."

Jordan smiled. "Enlighten us."

Nate smiled like a little kid. "What did the buffalo say when his kid went to college?"

Braxton, looking stumped, asked, "I don't know, what?"

Laughing, Nate said, "Bison."

Jordan shook his head and kept his eyes on the road, trying not to smile. Everyone else just rolled their eyes.

Finally, Jace said, "That was really dumb, Nate."

A few minutes later, when Jordan heard Jace say, "Uh, I think we have some company," he thought another dumb joke was coming.

"I'm sure we do," Jordan said sarcastically.

"No, I'm serious," Jace said, looking out the back window. "There's two black vans right behind your dad, and they're speeding up. I think they're going to ram him."

Jordan's eyes darted to the rearview mirror, and fear caught hold of him.

I have no idea how I'm going to get everyone out of this mess in one piece.

TO BE
CONTINUED

Acknowledgments

Wow! I cannot believe how many people have helped me with writing and publishing this book.

I would like to say, thank you, fellow readers for supporting this book. None of this would've been possible without your help!

I would also like to thank my Editor Christopher Bigelow, Book Cover Designer Rian Gordon, and Proofreading by Hannah G. Scheffer-Wentz, English Proper Editing Services.

I began writing the Grace's Life series when I was eleven years old, and have been working on it since then.

As I started my writing journey, I felt a lot of self-doubt about my dream to become an author. I felt that I wasn't that experienced in writing.

I would once again like to thank my parents for helping me with this very long journey. Helping me financially when I didn't have the money to pay for my book, mentally by encouraging me when I thought I couldn't keep going, and emotionally by listening to my frustrations and excitements. They have supported my idea of writing a book and being published since the day I began writing.

I would like to thank all of my other family members for asking about my book and taking an interest in it. Your encouragement and interest did not go unnoticed. I love you all so much.

I would like to thank my friends for supporting me as well. You gave me so much encouragement. And I know some of you have said from the very beginning that you'd buy my book once I publish it. Your constant support has helped me keep going. I love you all.

I would like to thank everyone that I've gotten feedback from. Especially my friends. Shout out to Emilee Iverson and Alex Kendall for reading all of the old versions of Grace's Life and giving such awesome feedback.

The inspiration that made me want to write a book in the first place, has come from books and music. I've read a lot of books in my life, but there are authors that have impacted or inspired me in some way.

I'd like to thank all of my English teachers that I've had all throughout my school years. Thank you for teaching me and pushing me to reach my full potential.

I have been able to achieve a very big dream of mine; writing a book that others can read as well. I want to let those of you who have doubts, you can do it. You can achieve anything!

You can prove to those who are putting you down. Prove that they're wrong. With a good mindset, you can do anything.

See you in the next adventure!

About the Author

MAKENZIE CARPENTER is a novelist, born and raised in Utah. She still resides in beautiful Utah with her family and her adorable little Yorkshire terrier. Makenzie will be pursuing a degree in American Sign Language Interpreting at a local Utah college. When not writing awesome Young Adult adventures, she can be found reading, talking about writing, baking, camping, or out in nature.

CONNECT WITH MAKENZIE ON:

Instagram: @author_makenziecarpenter

Made in United States
Troutdale, OR
03/28/2025

30126372R10173